DAY OF THE

FIELD TRIP ZOMBIES

Librarian Reviewer
Katharine Kan
Graphic novel reviewer and Library Consultant, Panama City, FL
MLS in Library and Information Studies, University of Hawaii at
Manoa, HI

Reading Consultant
Elizabeth Stedem
Educator/Consultant, Colorado Springs, CO
MA in Elementary Education, University of Denver, CO

STONE ARCH BOOKS
MINNEAPOLIS   SAN DIEGO

Graphic Sparks are published by Stone Arch Books
151 Good Counsel Drive, P.O. Box 669
Mankato, Minnesota 56002
www.stonearchbooks.com

Library of Congress Cataloging-in-Publication Data
Nickel, Scott.
Day of the Field Trip Zombies / by Scott Nickel; illustrated by Cedric Hohnstadt.
p. cm. — (Graphic Sparks. School Zombies)
ISBN-13: 978-1-59889-834-7 (library binding)
ISBN-10: 1-59889-834-5 (library binding)
ISBN-13: 978-1-59889-890-3 (paperback)
ISBN-10: 1-59889-890-6 (paperback)
1. Graphic novels. I. Hohnstadt, Cedric. II. Title.
PN6727.N544D39 2008
741.5'973—dc22 2007003175

Summary: Trevor is an expert on zombies. In fact, he's a zombie-buster. When his class takes a field trip to an aquarium, the evil scientist Dr. Brainium turns the students into radio-controlled zombies. Only Trevor can rescue them, but first he has to escape an army of psycho penguins!

Art Director: Heather Kindseth
Graphic Designer: Brann Garvey

Printed in the United States of America

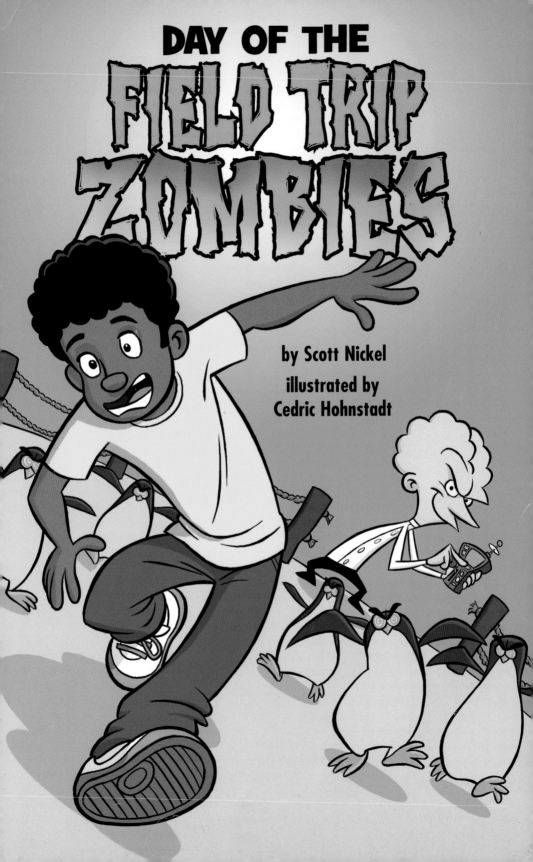

DAY OF THE FIELD TRIP ZOMBIES

by Scott Nickel

illustrated by
Cedric Hohnstadt

CAST OF CHARACTERS

TREVOR WALTON

CAPTAIN STEVE

MR. DEAN

DR. BRAINIUM

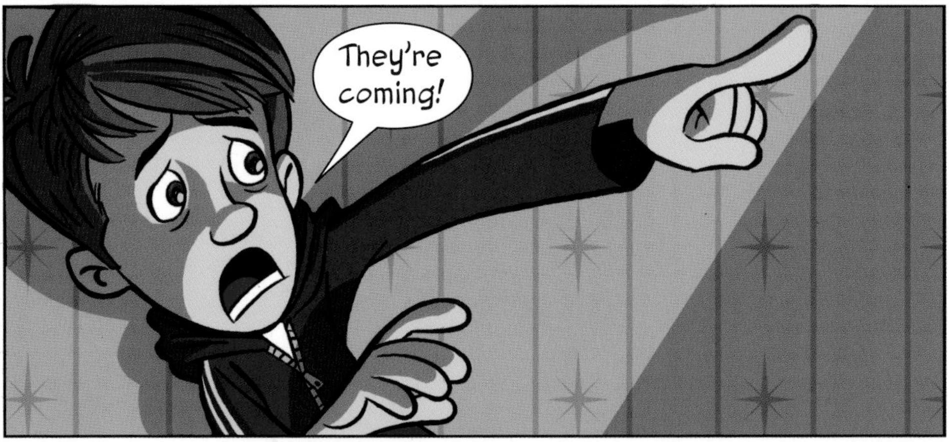
They're coming!

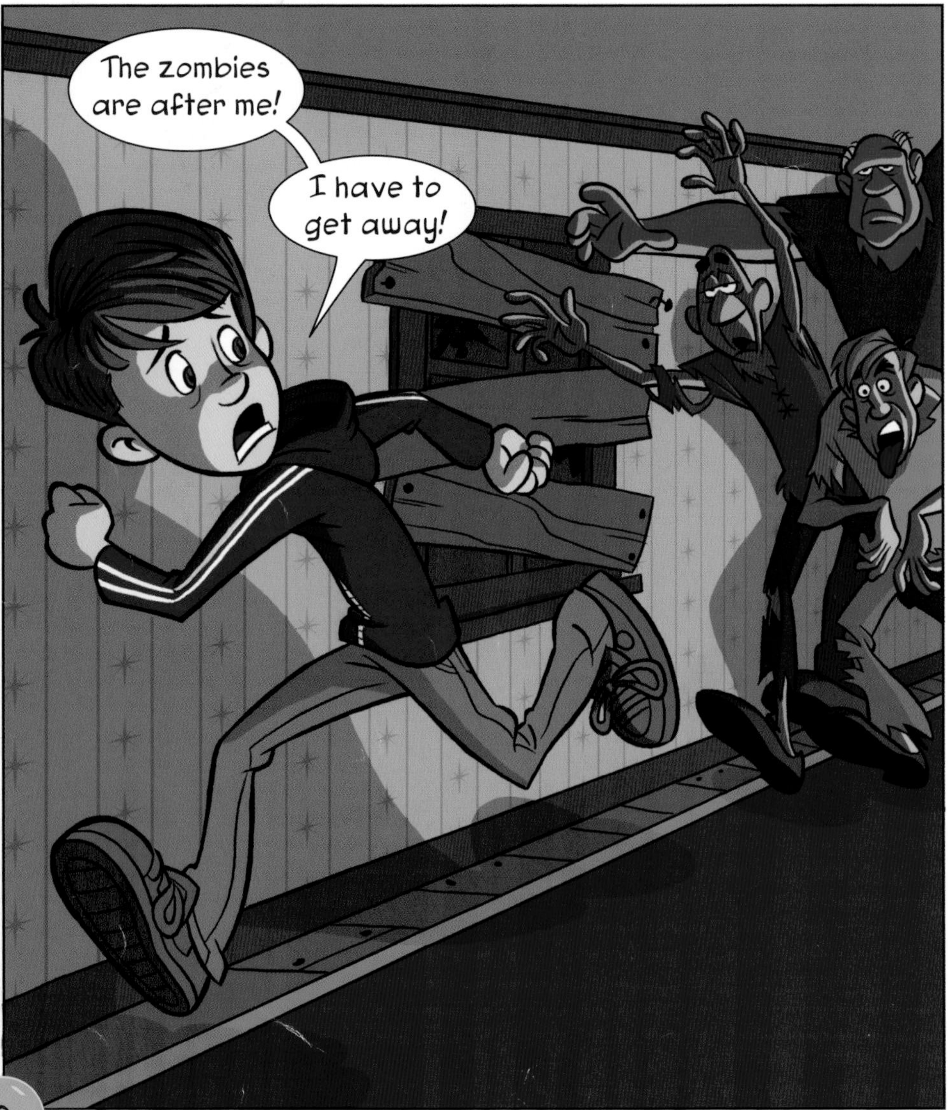
The zombies are after me!
I have to get away!

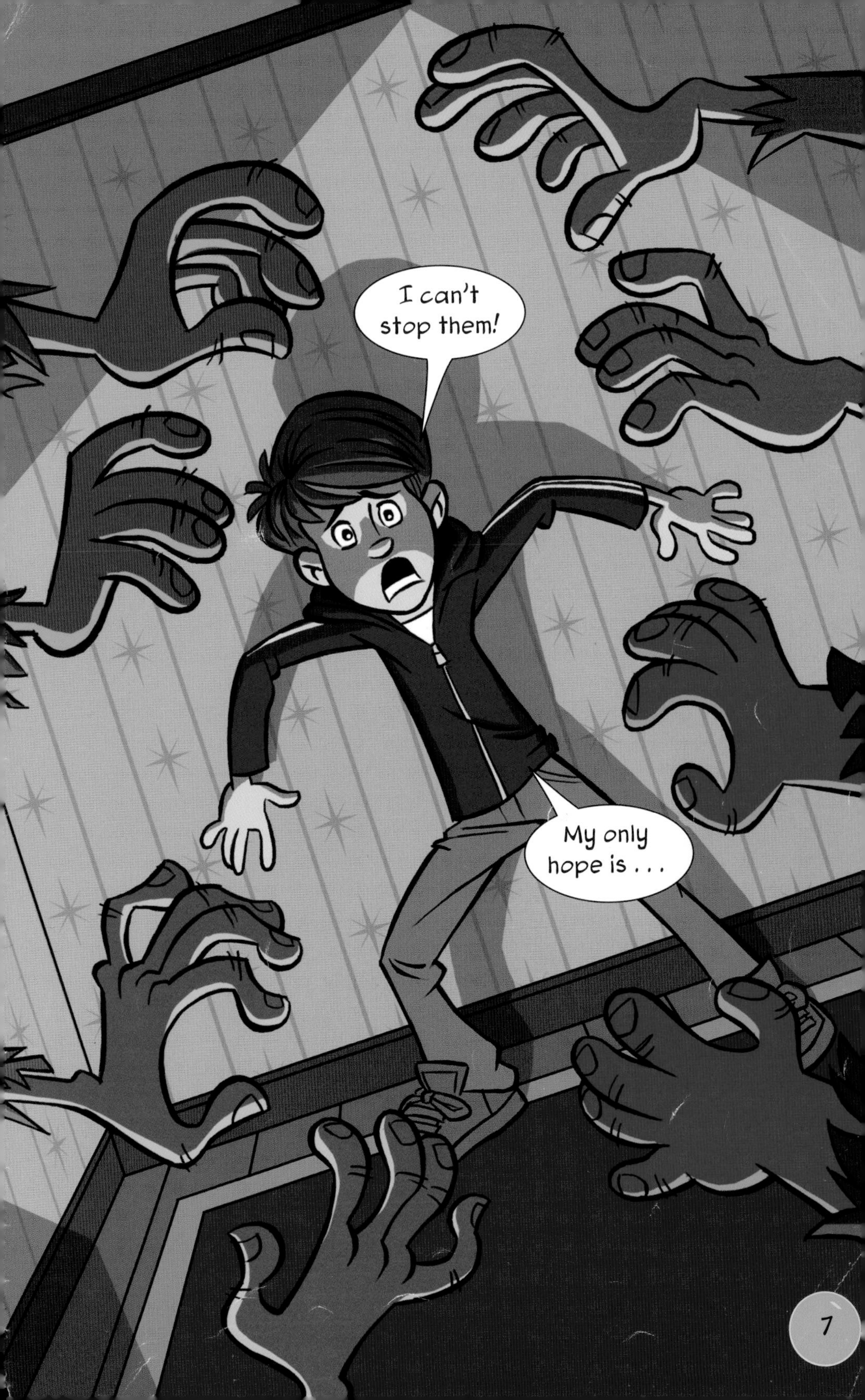
I can't stop them!
My only hope is . . .

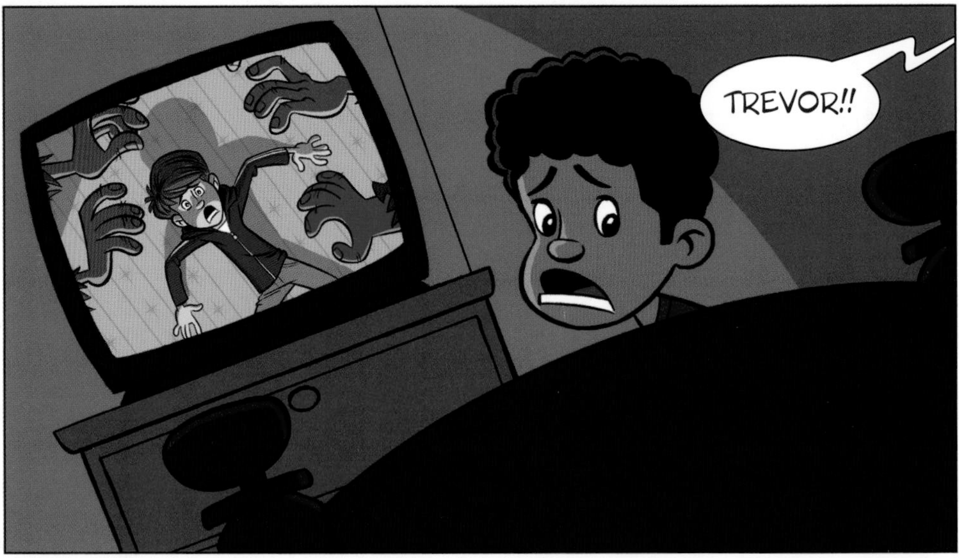
TREVOR!!

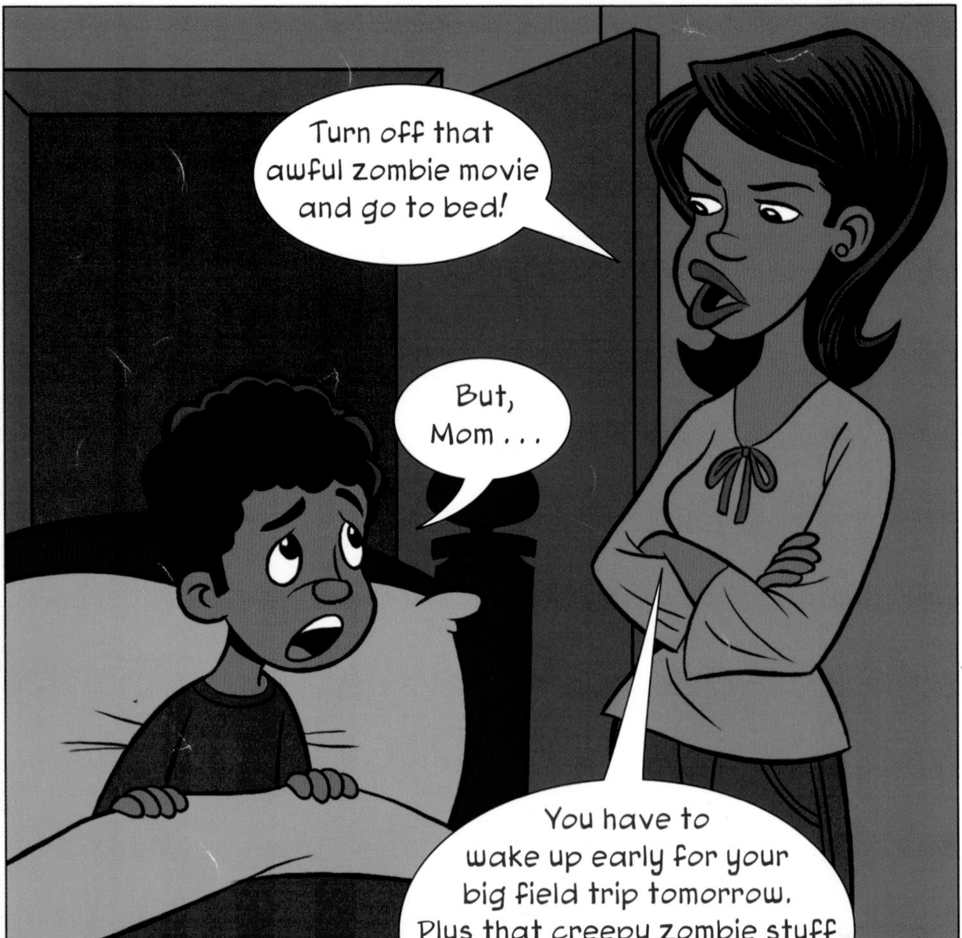
Turn off that awful zombie movie and go to bed!
But, Mom . . .
You have to wake up early for your big field trip tomorrow. Plus that creepy zombie stuff will give you nightmares.

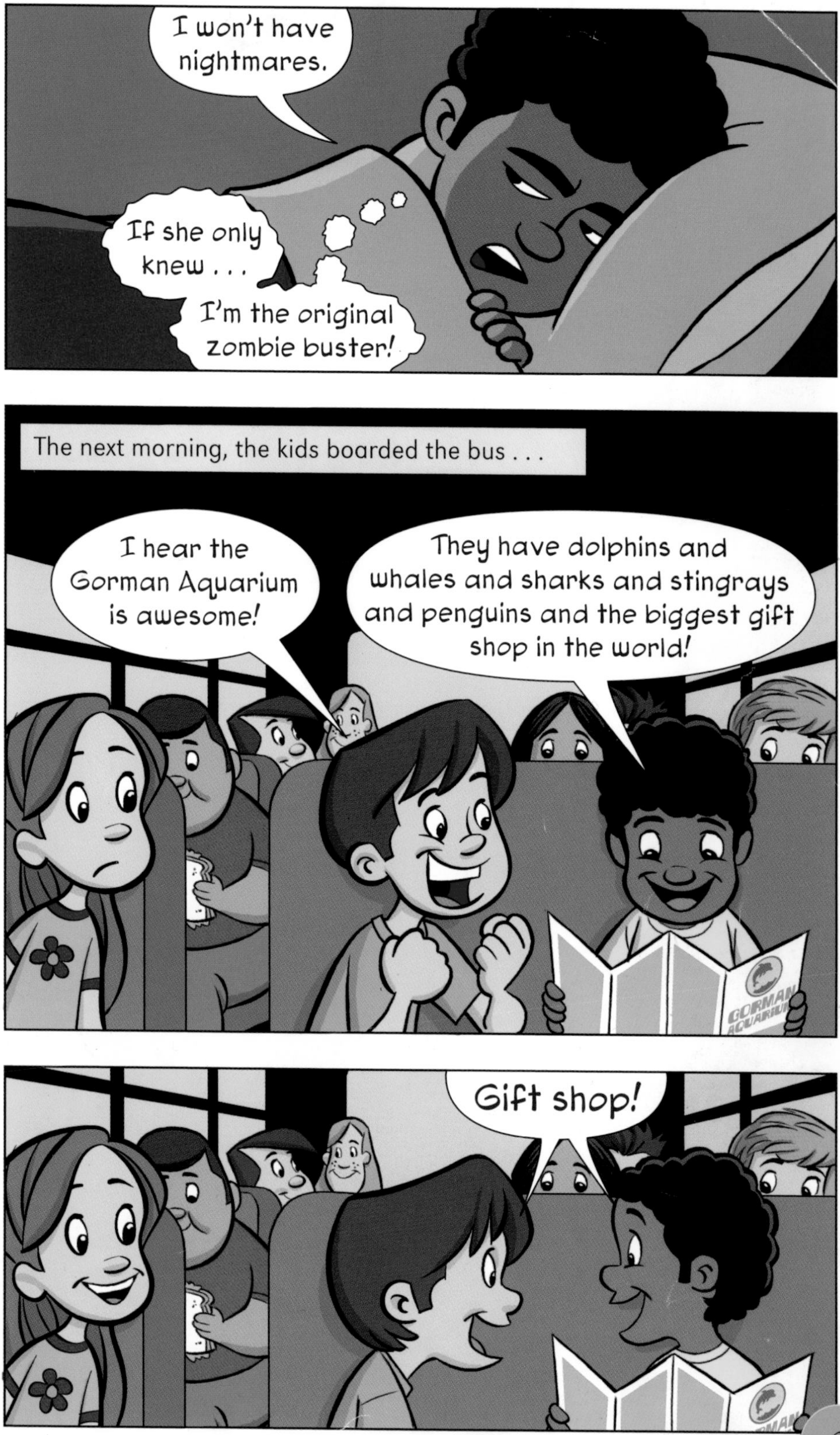
I won't have nightmares.
If she only knew . . .
I'm the original zombie buster!
The next morning, the kids boarded the bus . . .
I hear the Gorman Aquarium is awesome!
They have dolphins and whales and sharks and stingrays and penguins and the biggest gift shop in the world!
Gift shop!

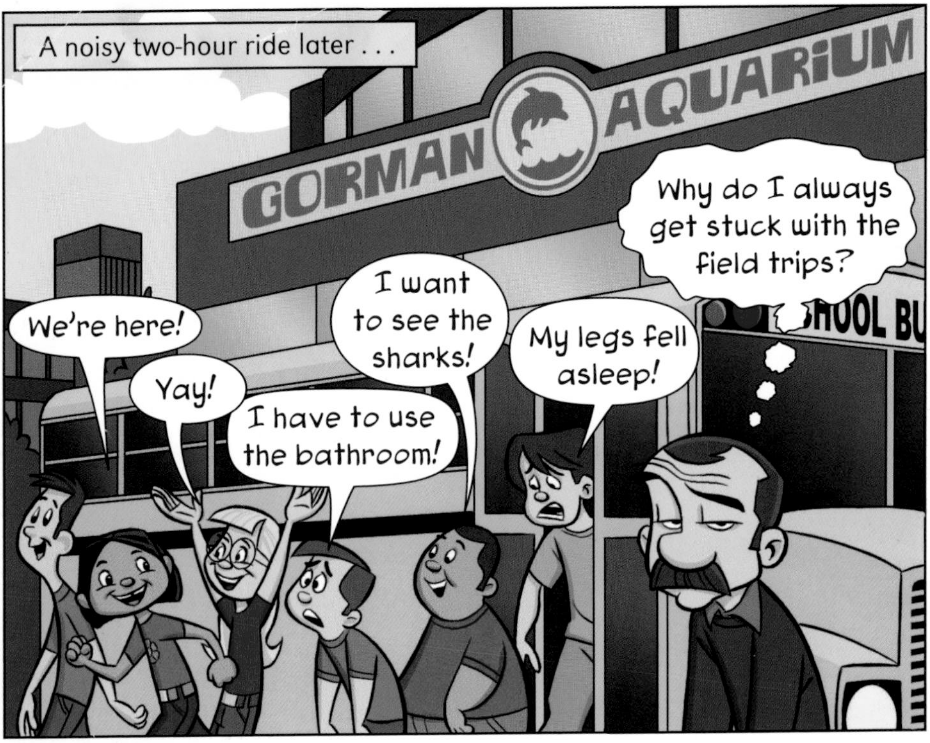
A noisy two-hour ride later . . .
GORMAN AQUARiUM
We're here!
Yay!
I have to use the bathroom!
I want to see the sharks!
My legs fell asleep!
Why do I always get stuck with the field trips?

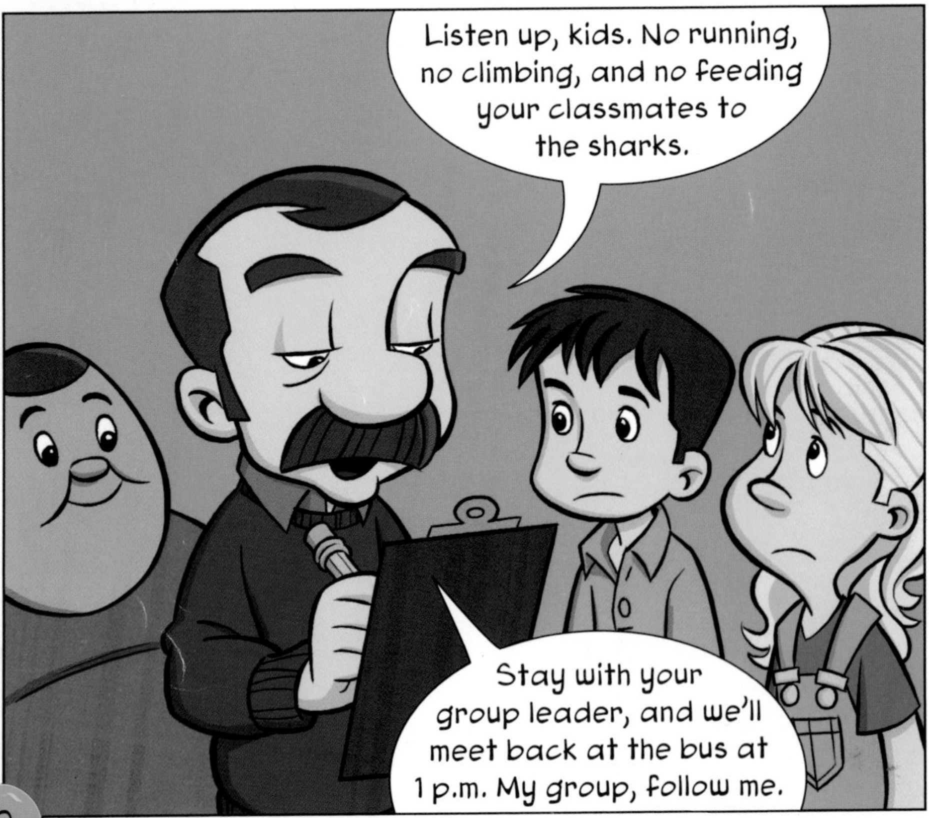
Listen up, kids. No running, no climbing, and no feeding your classmates to the sharks.
Stay with your group leader, and we'll meet back at the bus at 1 p.m. My group, follow me.

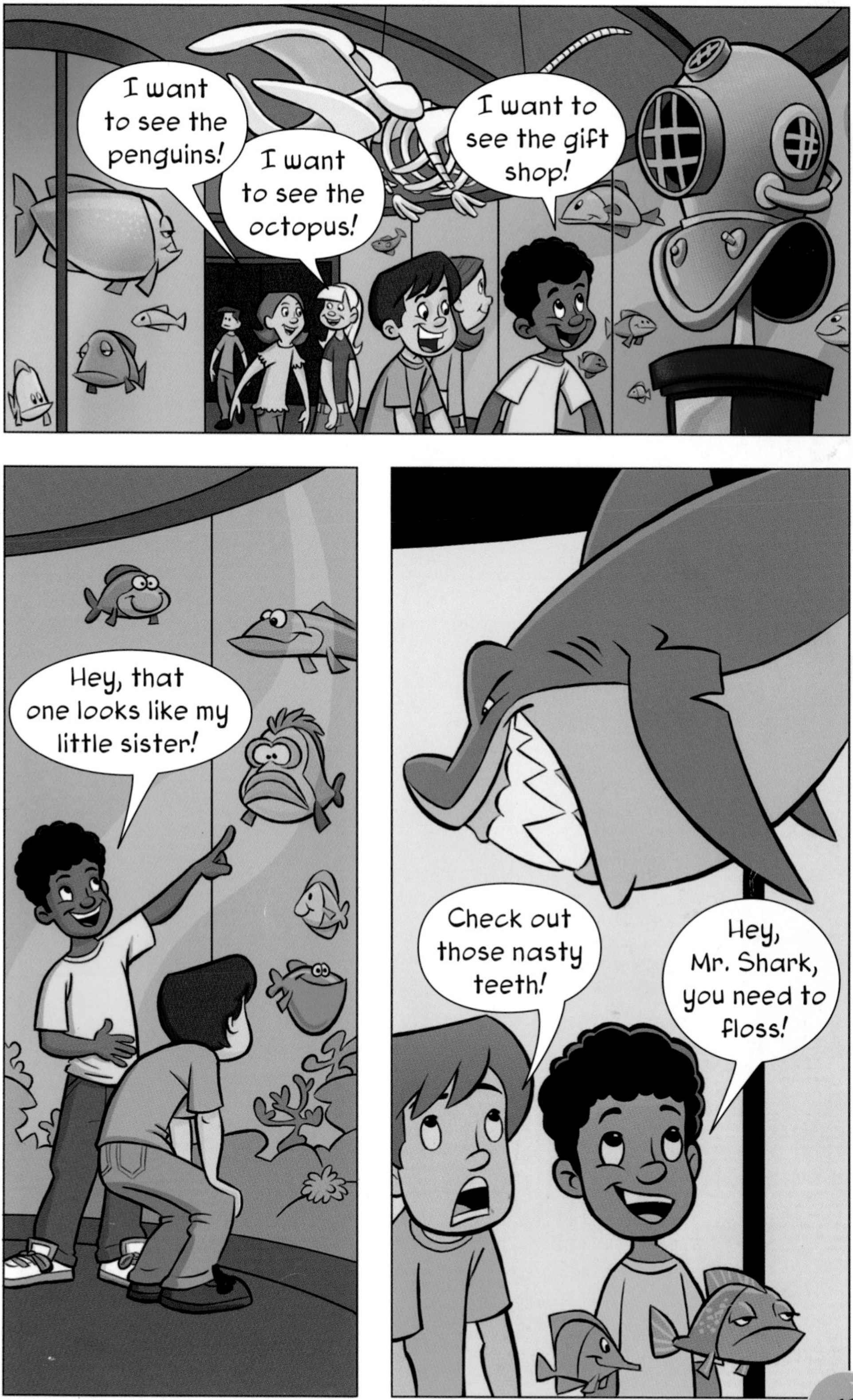
I want to see the penguins!
I want to see the octopus!
I want to see the gift shop!
Hey, that one looks like my little sister!
Check out those nasty teeth!
Hey, Mr. Shark, you need to floss!

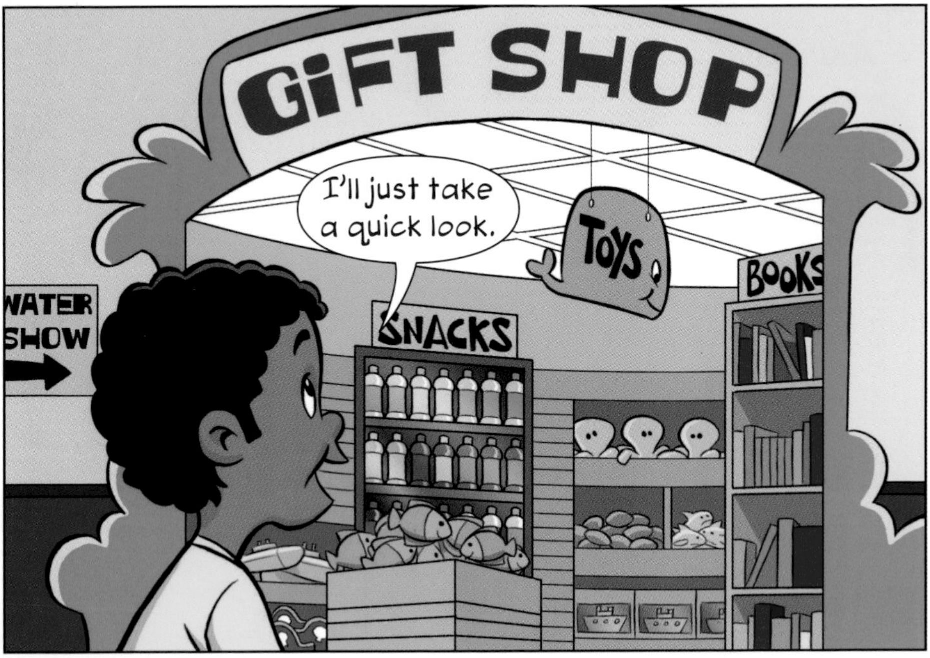
GIFT SHOP
I'll just take a quick look.
TOYS
BOOKS
WATER SHOW
SNACKS

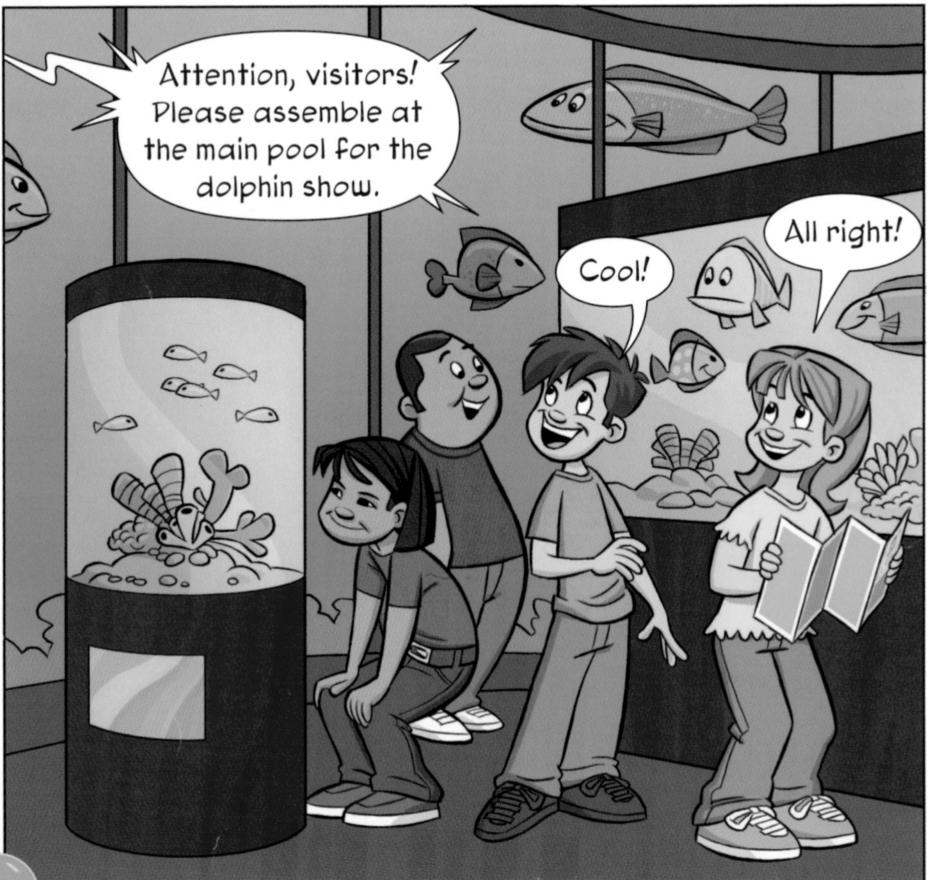
Attention, visitors! Please assemble at the main pool for the dolphin show.
Cool!
All right!

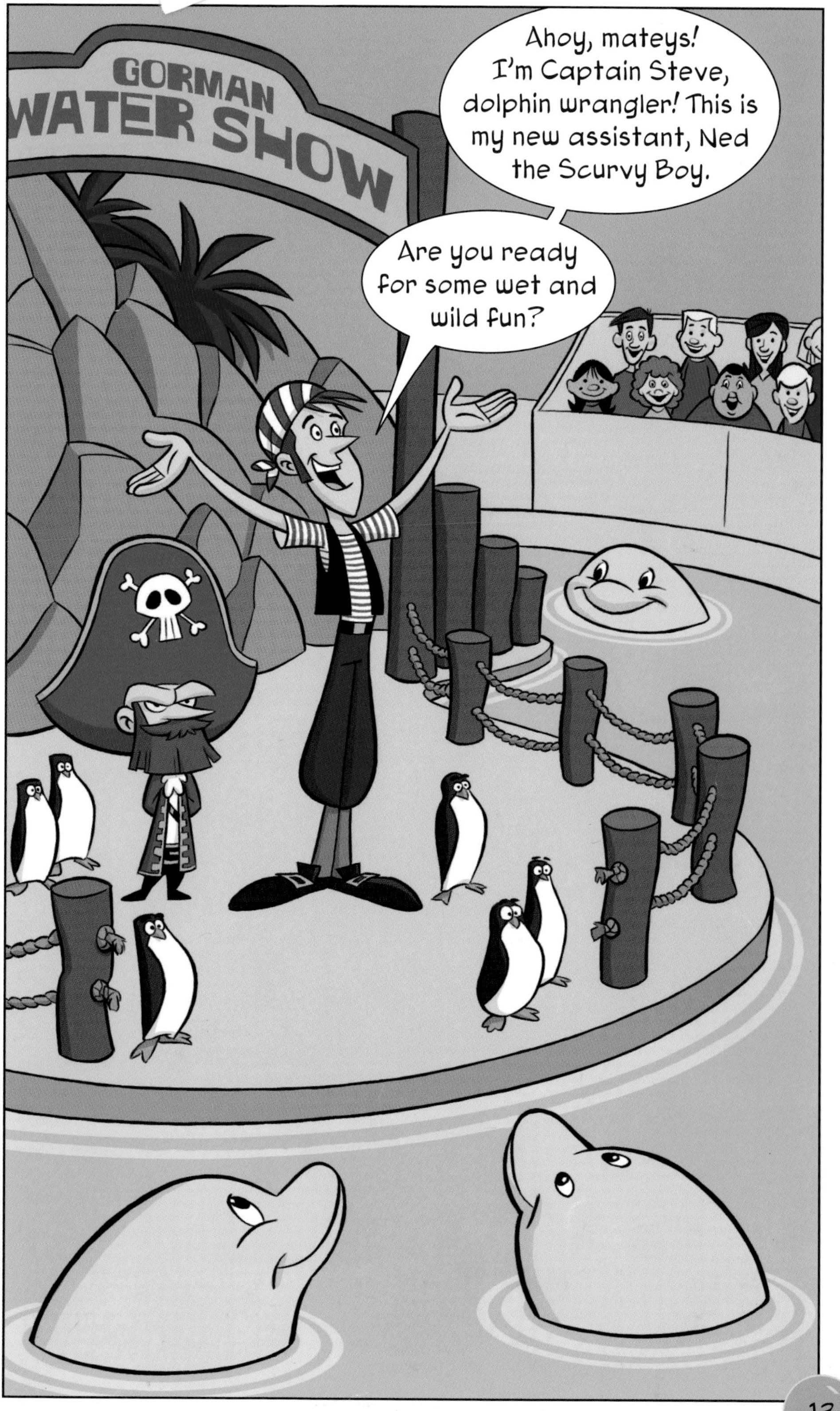
GORMAN WATER SHOW
Ahoy, mateys! I'm Captain Steve, dolphin wrangler! This is my new assistant, Ned the Scurvy Boy.
Are you ready for some wet and wild fun?

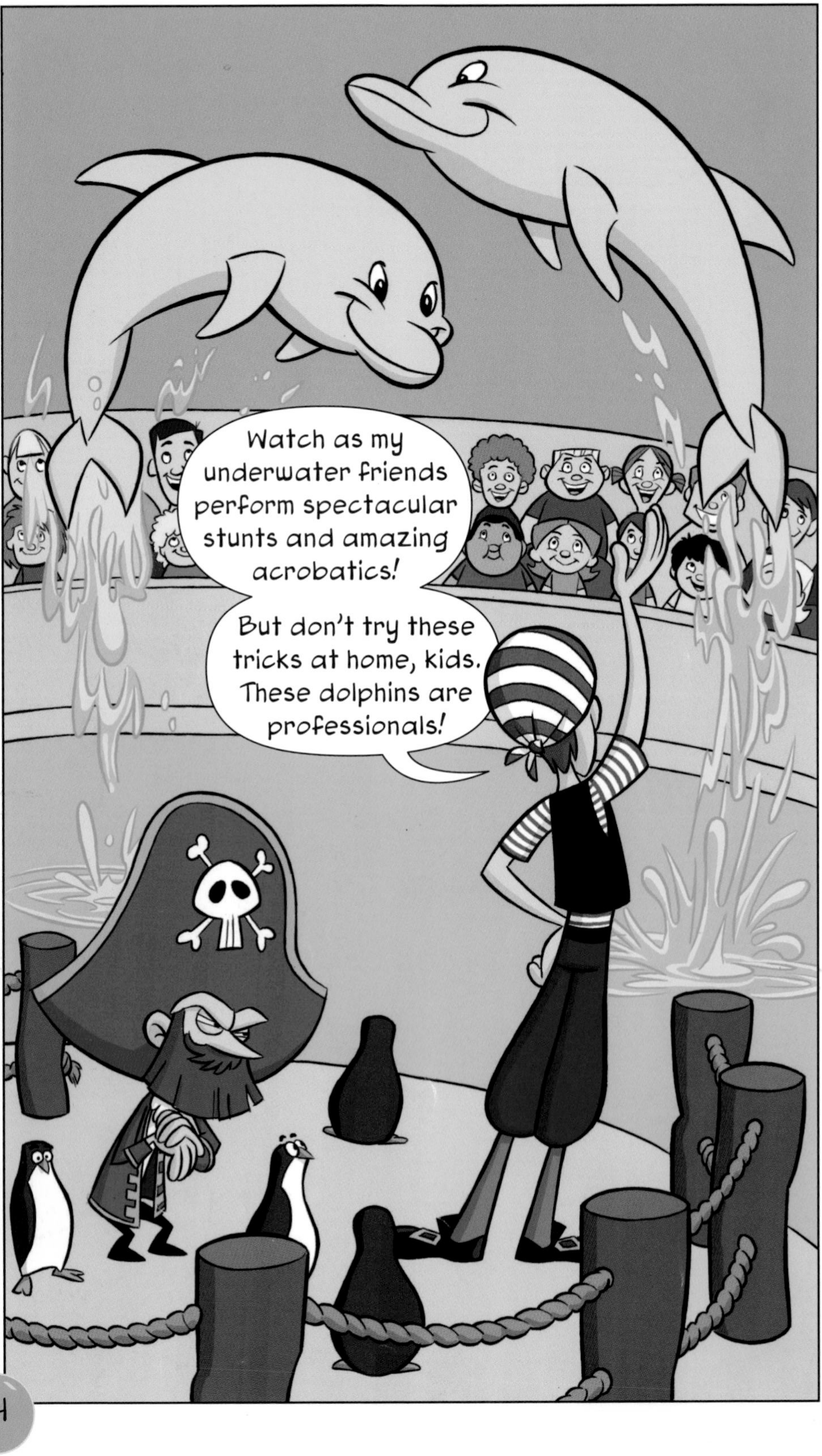
Watch as my underwater friends perform spectacular stunts and amazing acrobatics!
But don't try these tricks at home, kids. These dolphins are professionals!

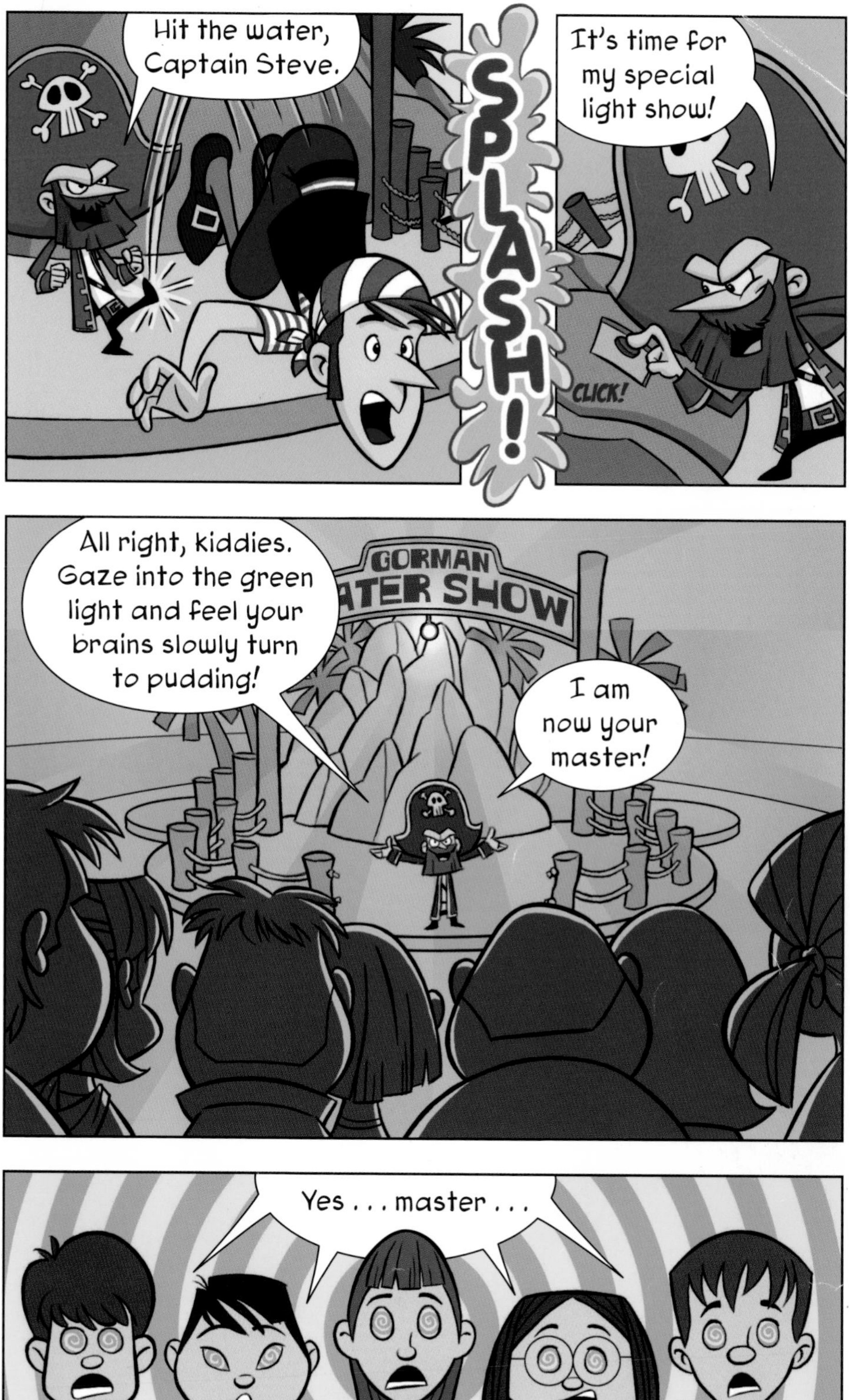
Hit the water, Captain Steve.
SPLASH!
It's time for my special light show!
CLICK!
GORMAN
ATER SHOW
All right, kiddies. Gaze into the green light and feel your brains slowly turn to pudding!
I am now your master!
Yes . . . master . . .

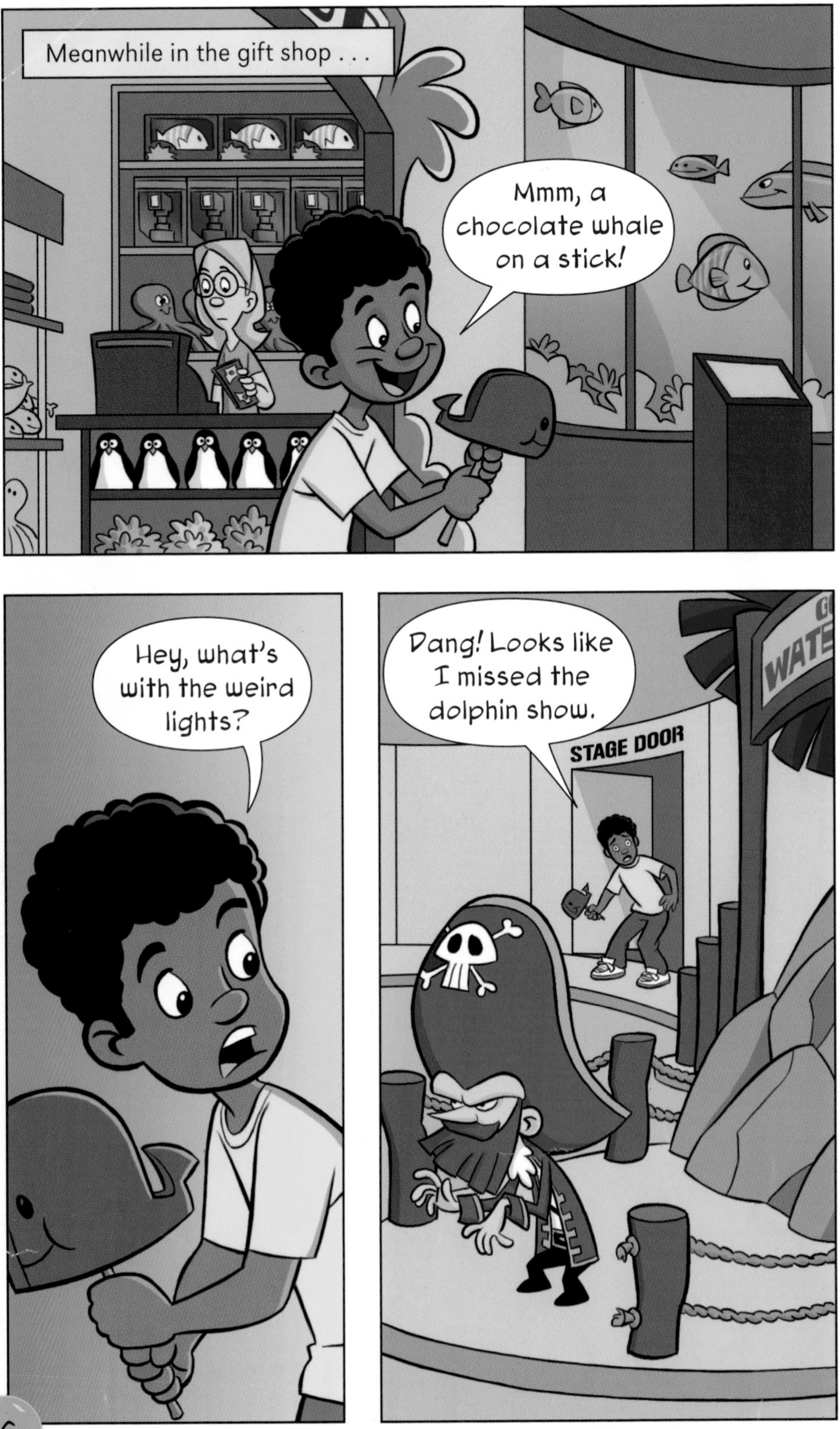
Meanwhile in the gift shop . . .
Mmm, a chocolate whale on a stick!
Hey, what's with the weird lights?
Dang! Looks like I missed the dolphin show.
STAGE DOOR

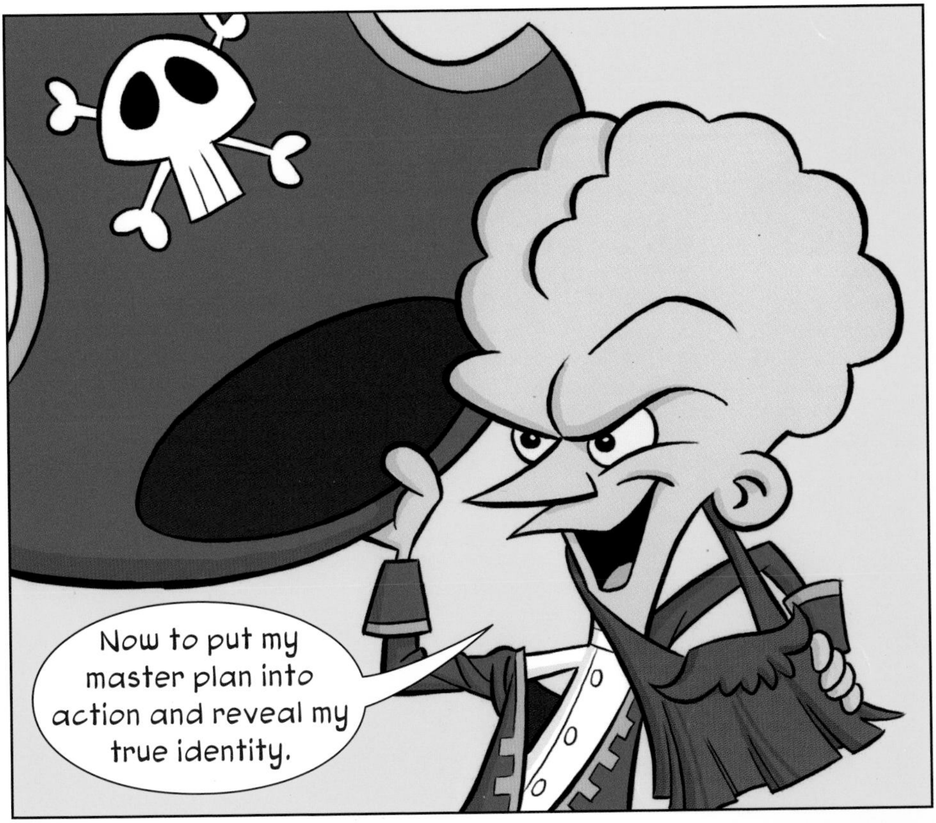
Now to put my master plan into action and reveal my true identity.

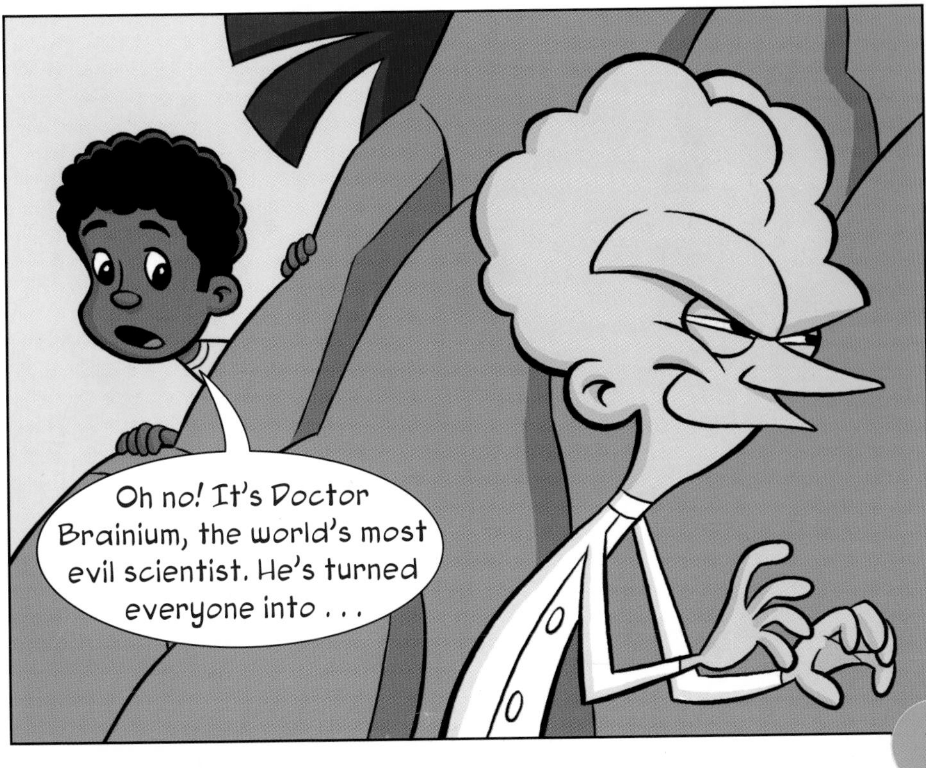
Oh no! It's Doctor Brainium, the world's most evil scientist. He's turned everyone into . . .

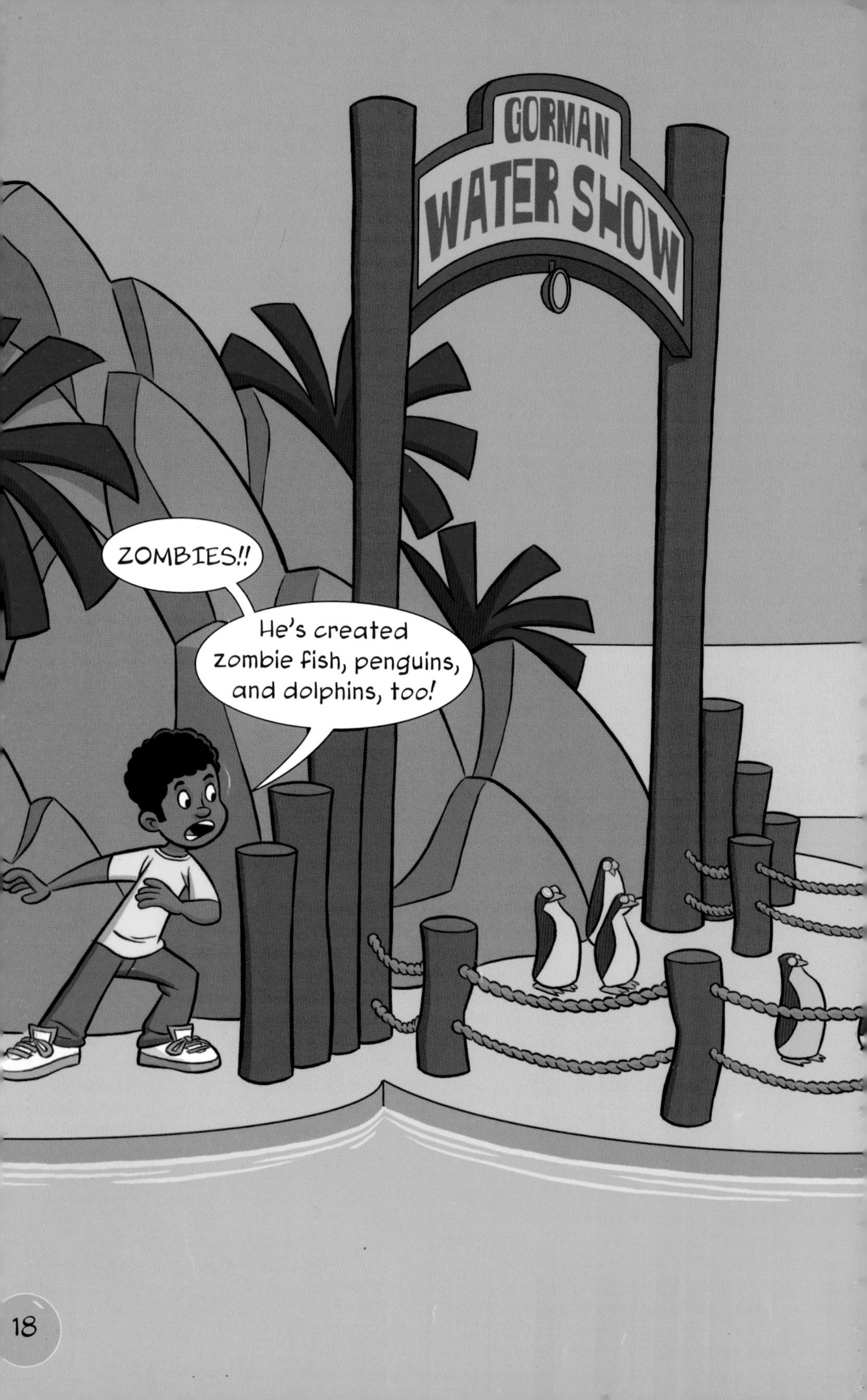
GORMAN
WATER SHOW
ZOMBIES!!
He's created zombie fish, penguins, and dolphins, too!

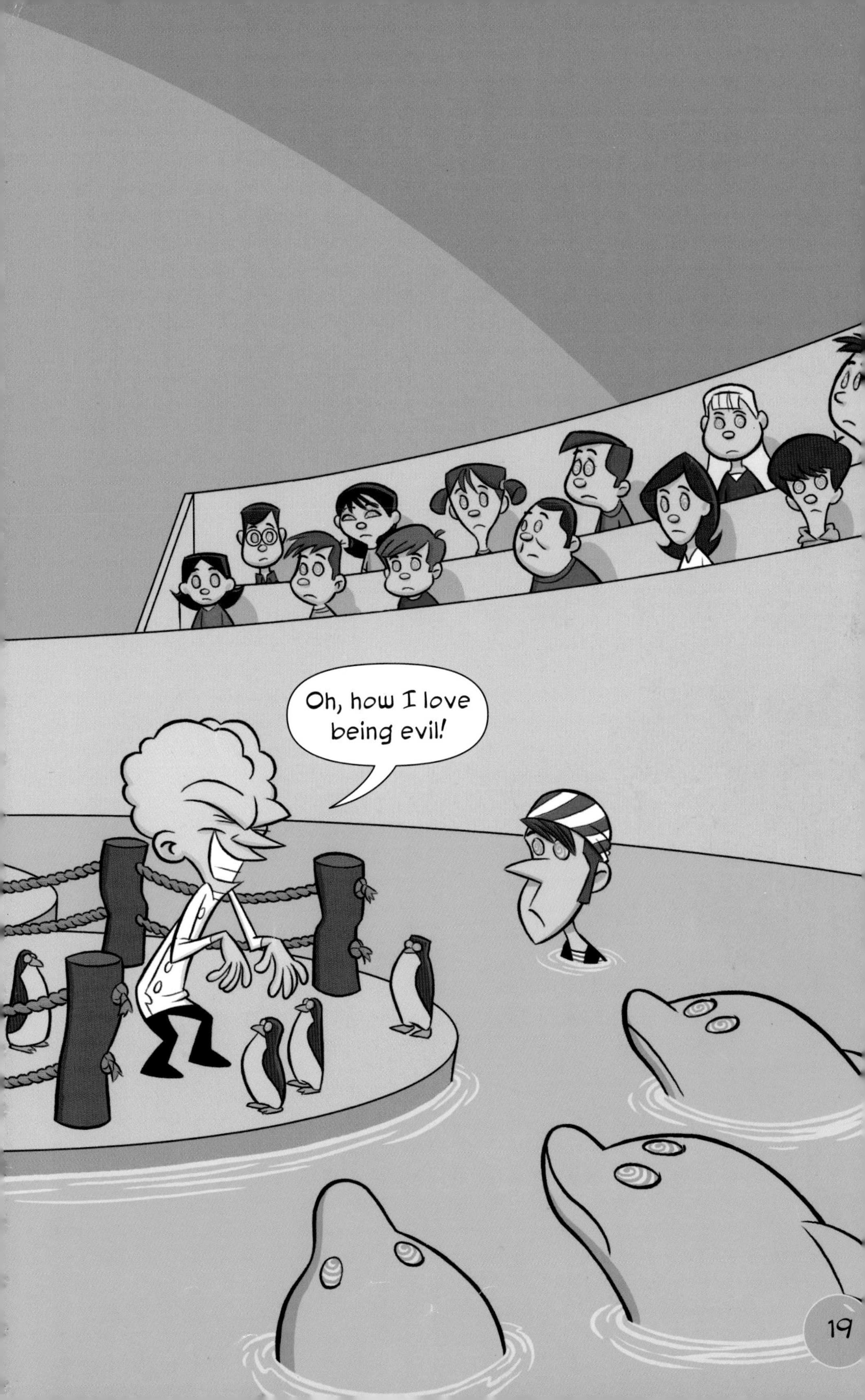
Oh, how I love being evil!

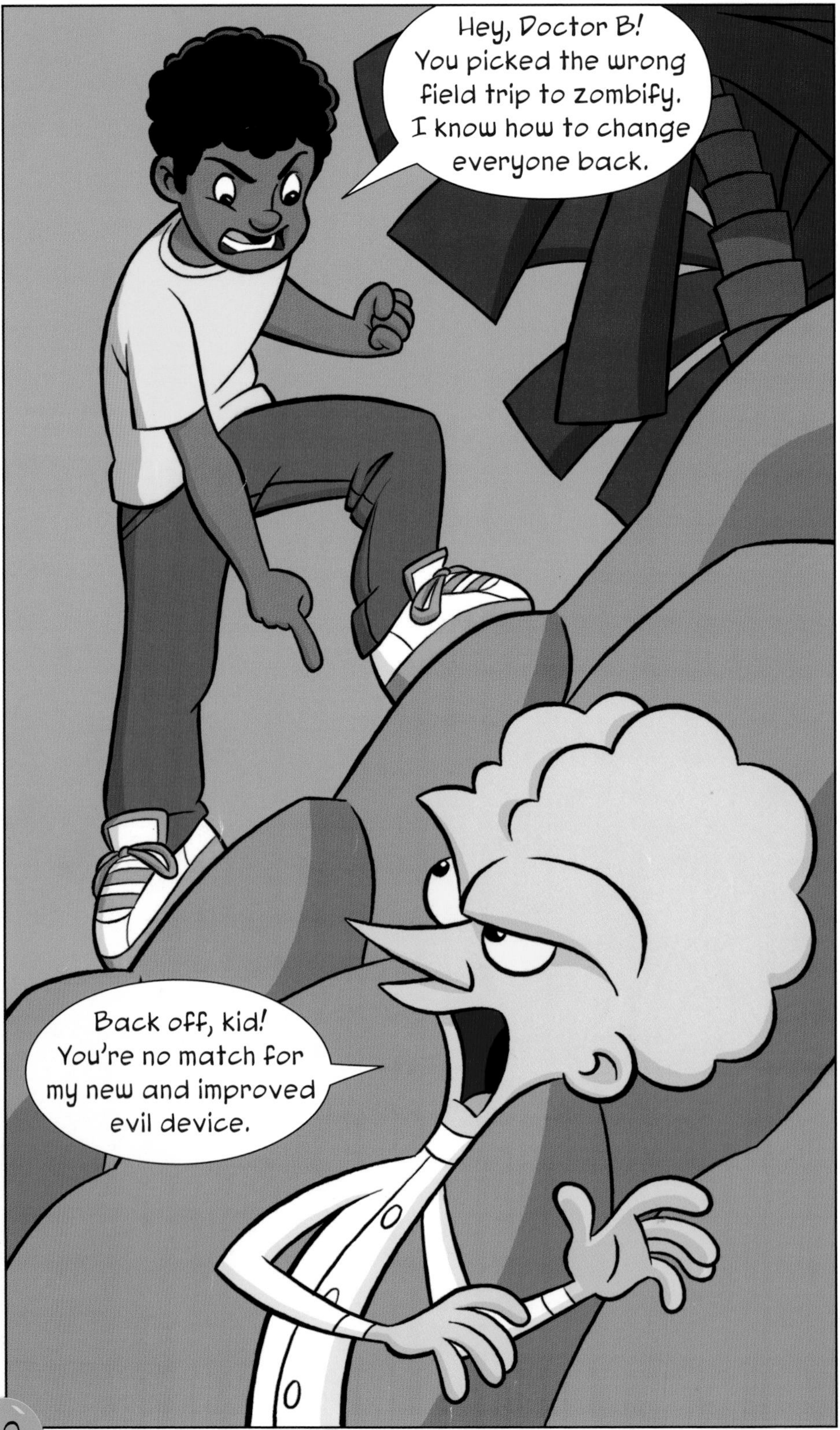
Hey, Doctor B! You picked the wrong field trip to zombify. I know how to change everyone back.
Back off, kid! You're no match for my new and improved evil device.

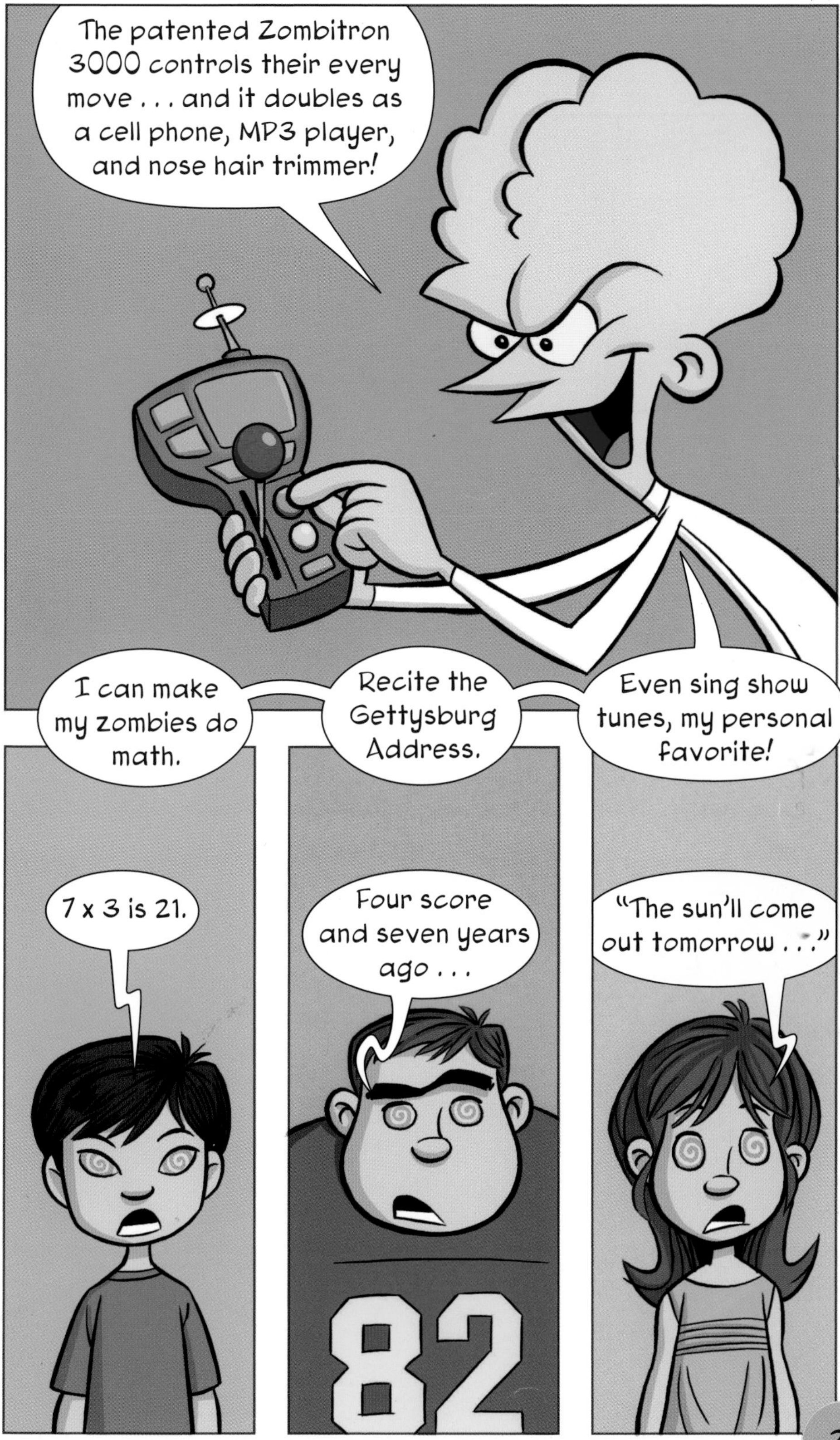
The patented Zombitron 3000 controls their every move . . . and it doubles as a cell phone, MP3 player, and nose hair trimmer!
I can make my zombies do math.
Recite the Gettysburg Address.
Even sing show tunes, my personal favorite!
7 x 3 is 21.
Four score and seven years ago . . .
"The sun'll come out tomorrow . . ."
82

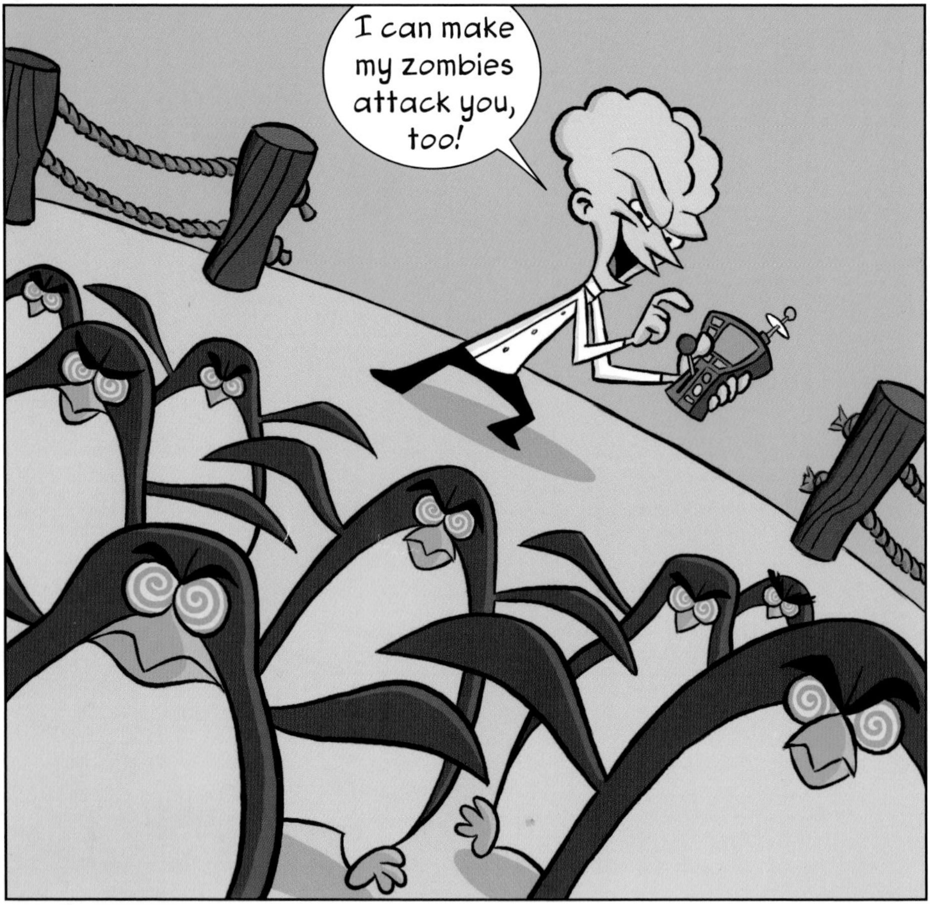
I can make my zombies attack you, too!

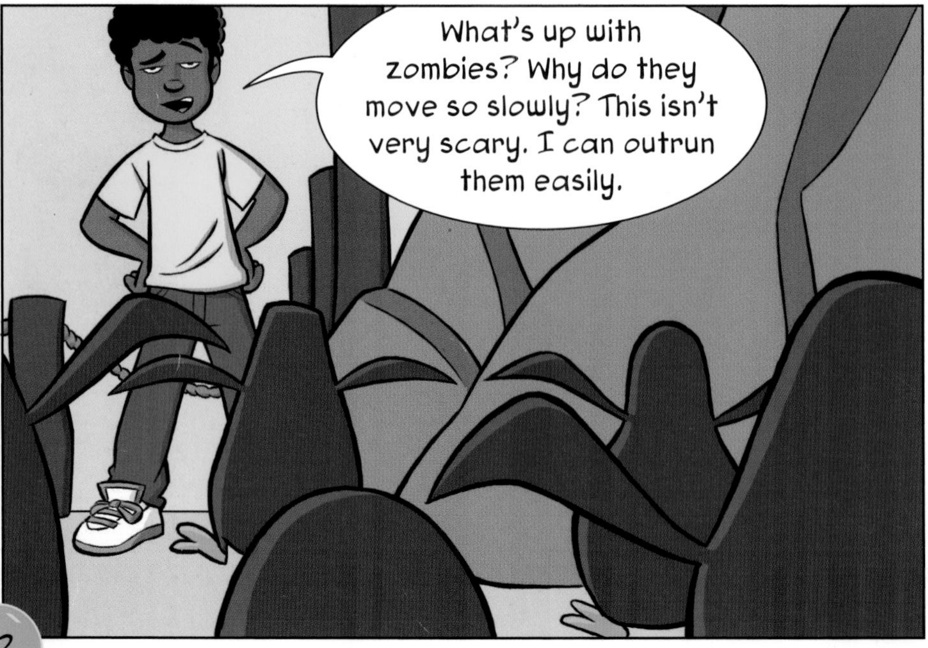
What's up with zombies? Why do they move so slowly? This isn't very scary. I can outrun them easily.

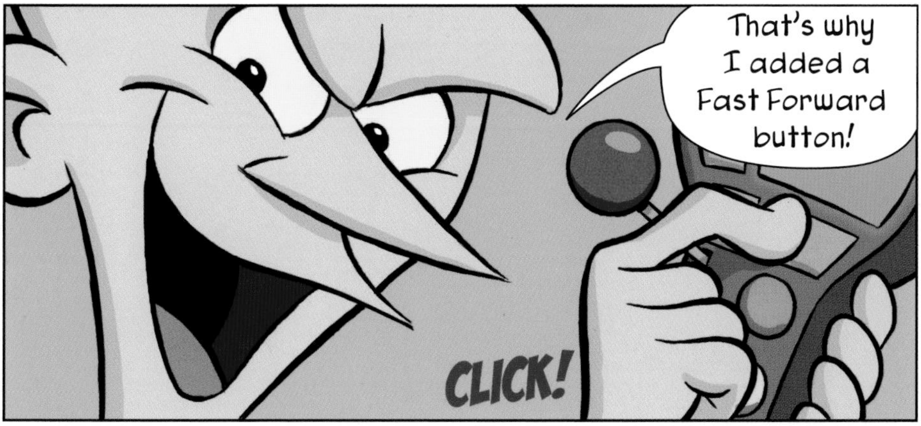
That's why I added a Fast Forward button!
CLICK!

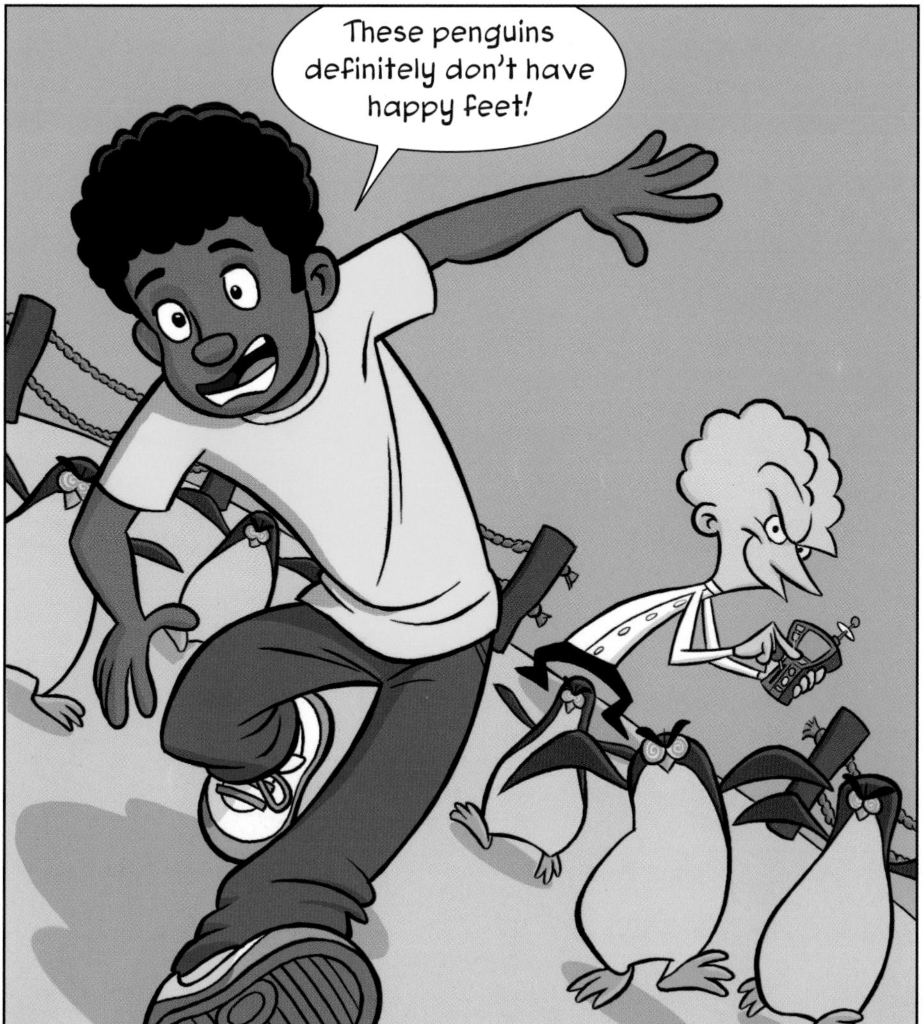
These penguins definitely don't have happy feet!

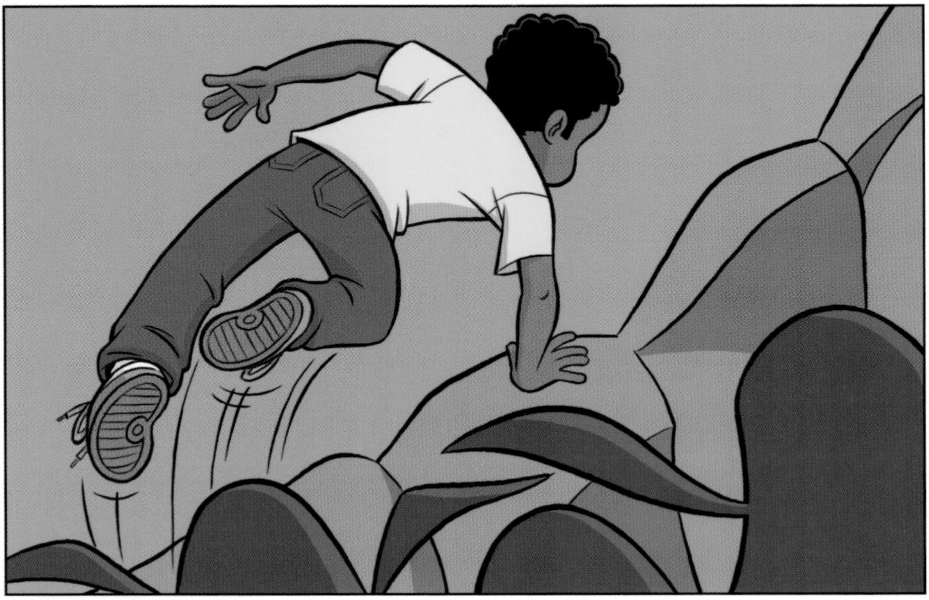

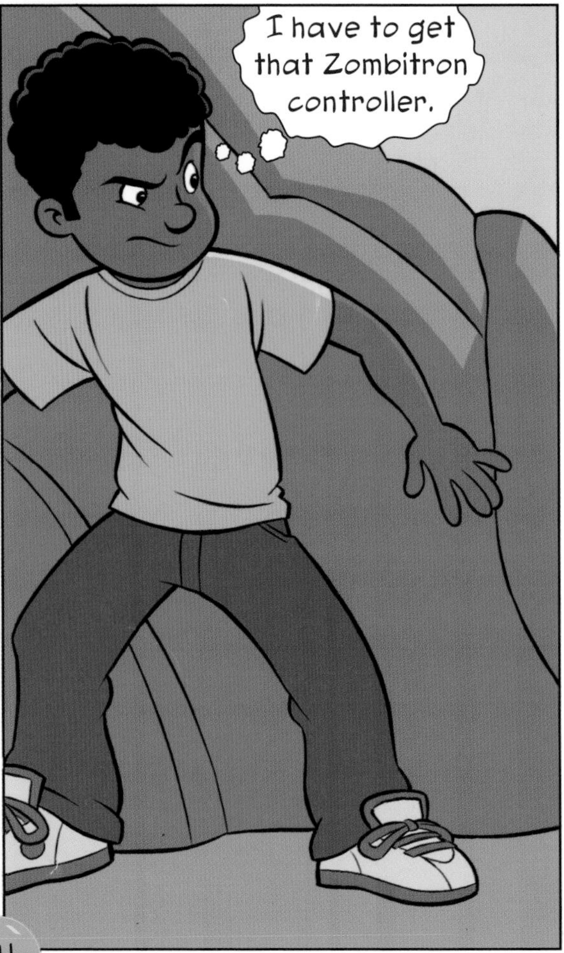
I have to get that Zombitron controller.

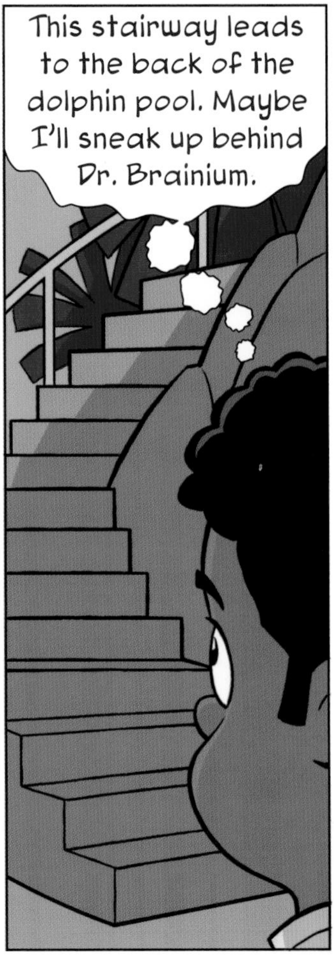
This stairway leads to the back of the dolphin pool. Maybe I'll sneak up behind Dr. Brainium.

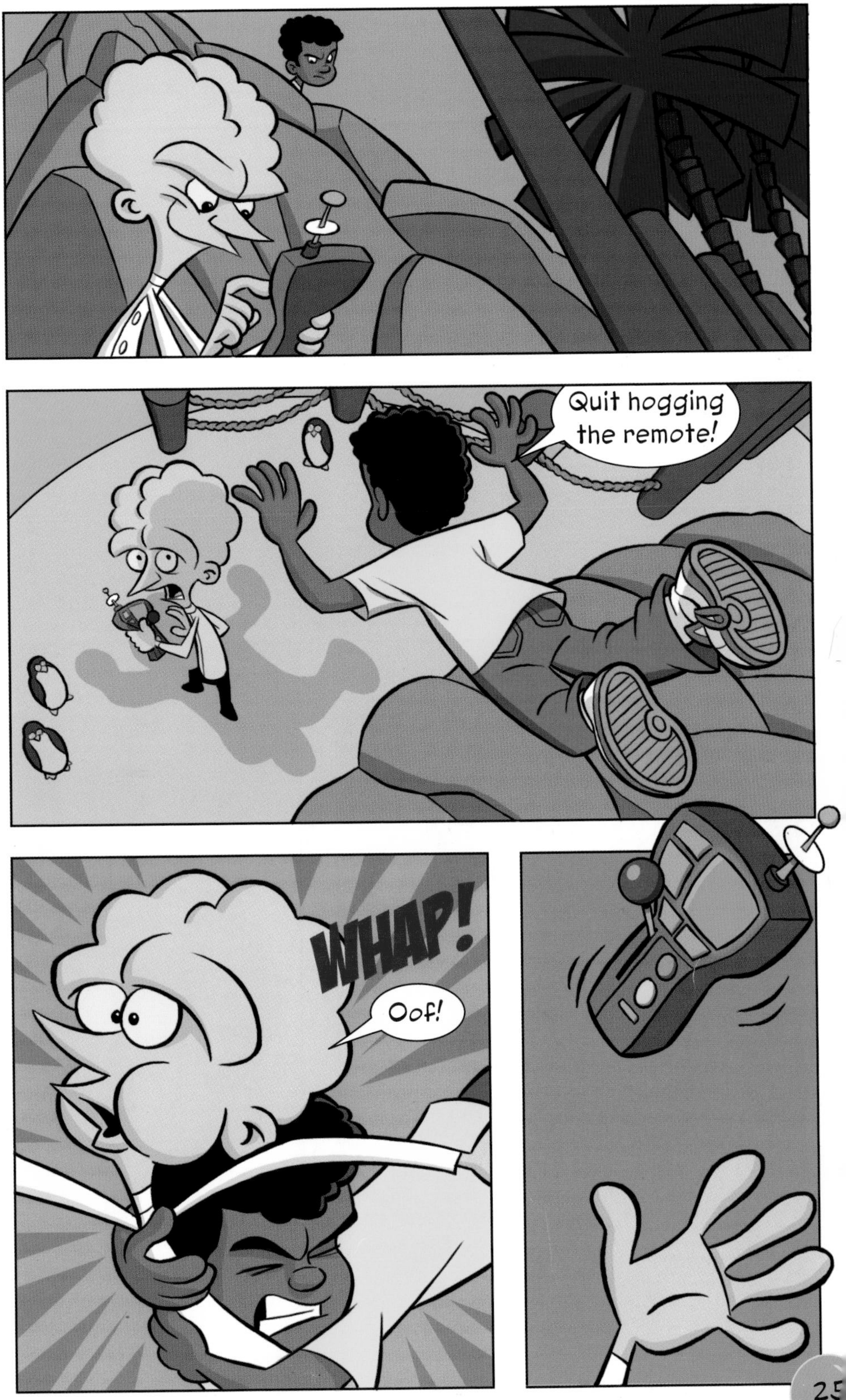
Quit hogging the remote!
WHAP!
Oof!

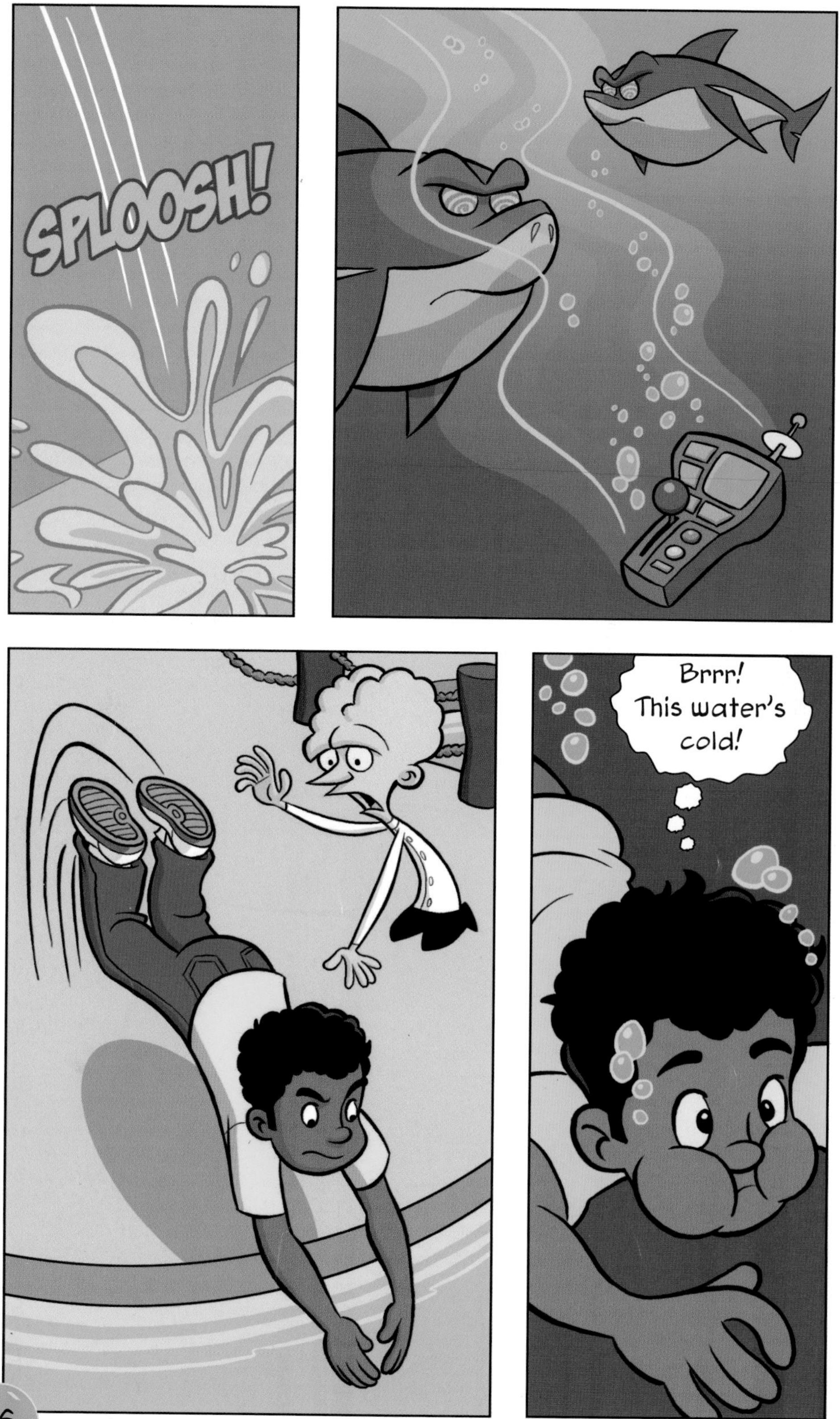
SPLOOSH!
Brrr! This water's cold!

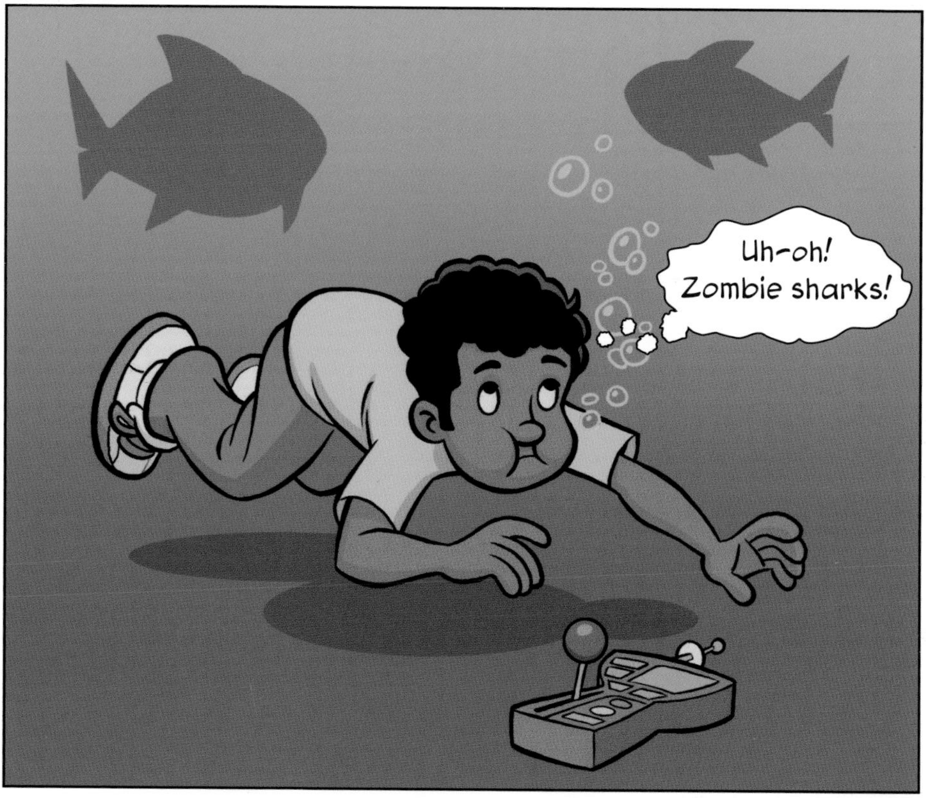
Uh-oh! Zombie sharks!

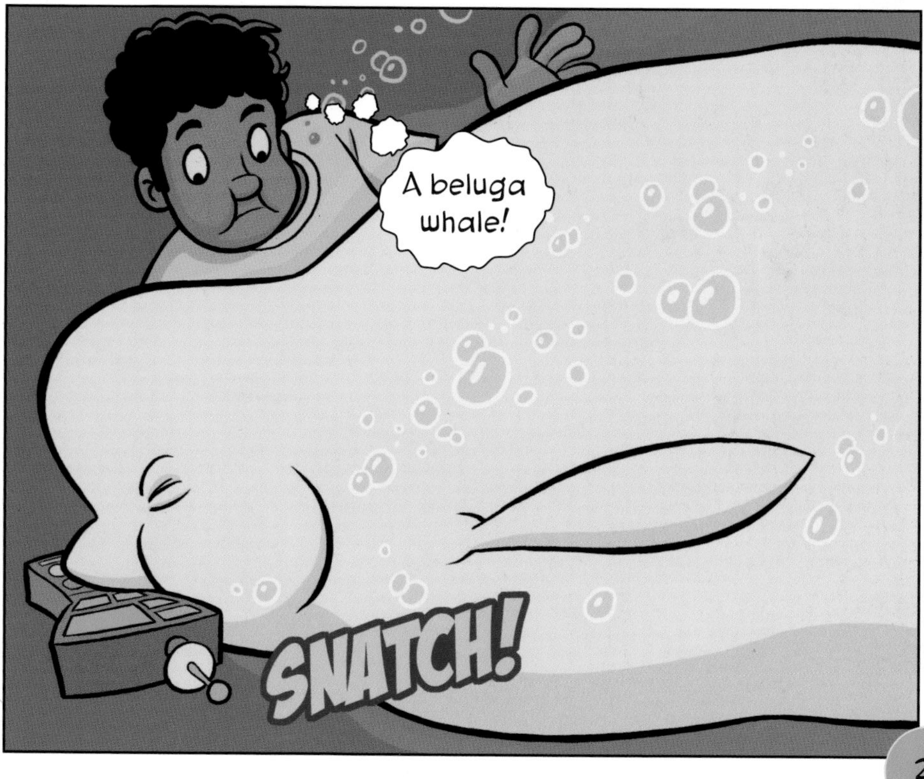
A beluga whale!
SNATCH!

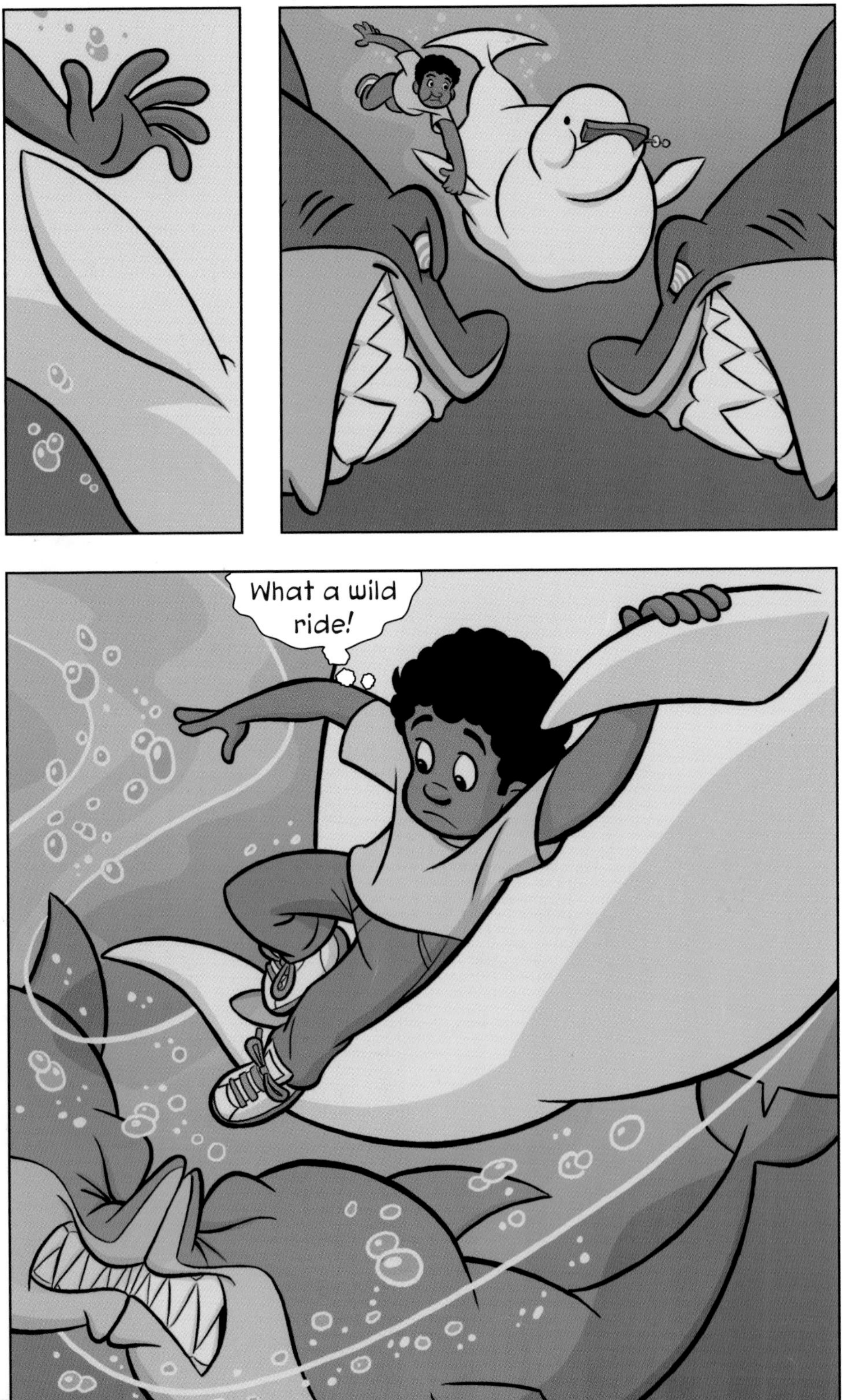
What a wild ride!

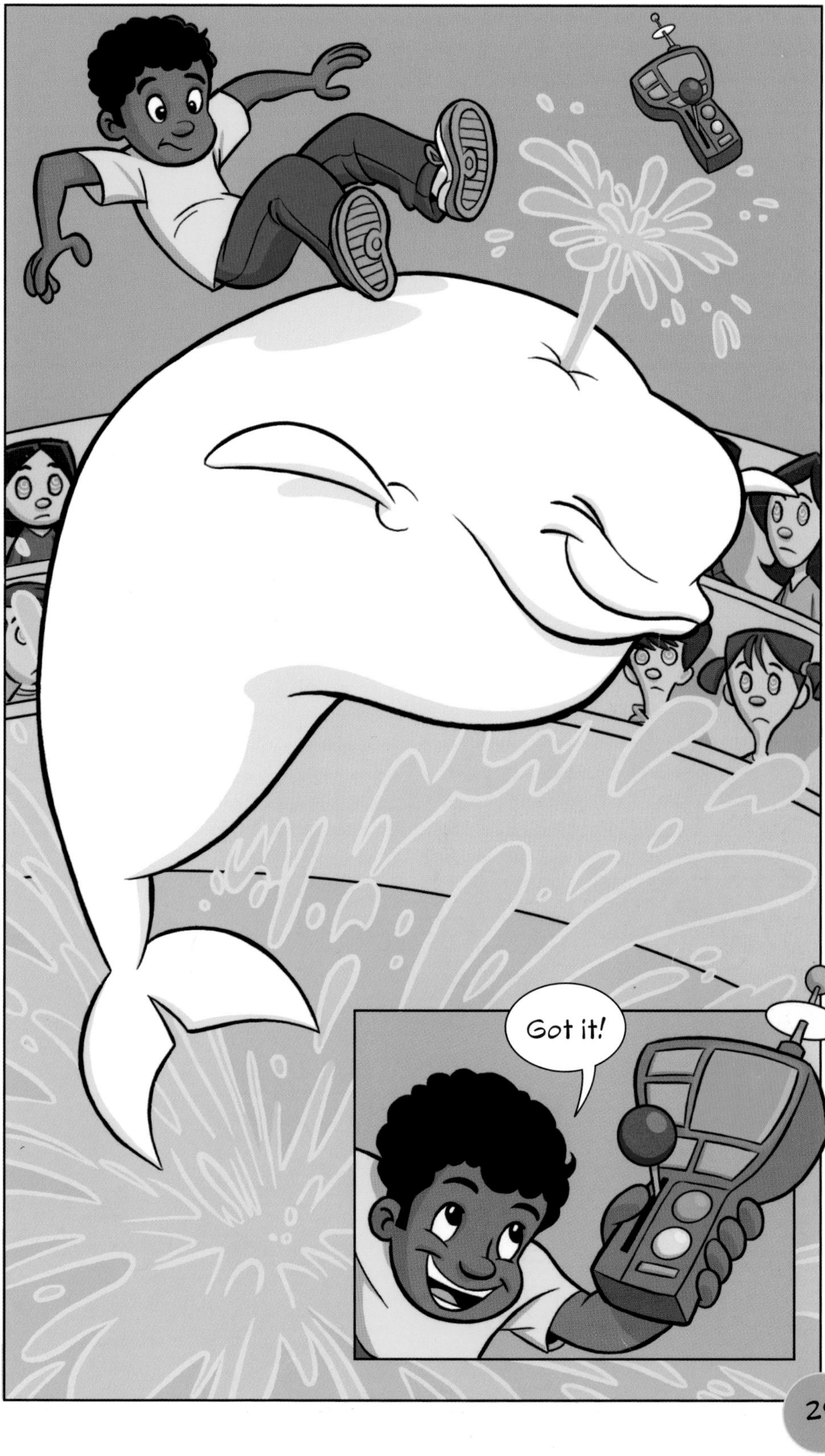
Got it!

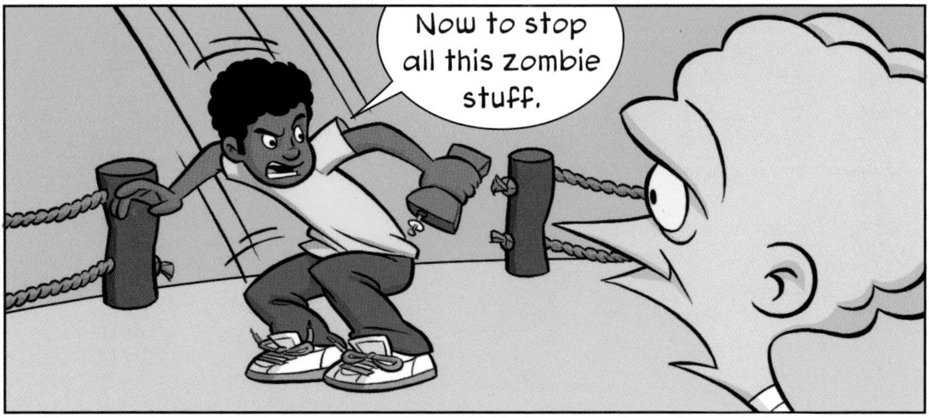
Now to stop all this zombie stuff.

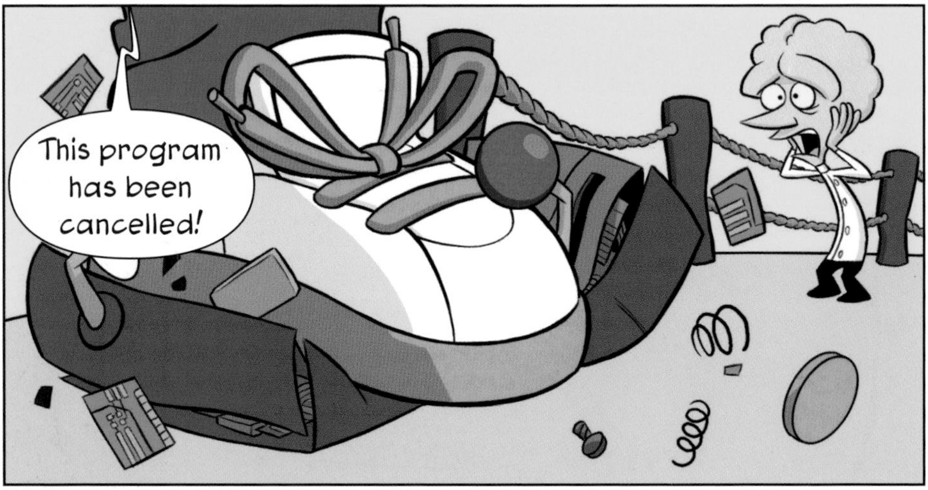
This program has been cancelled!

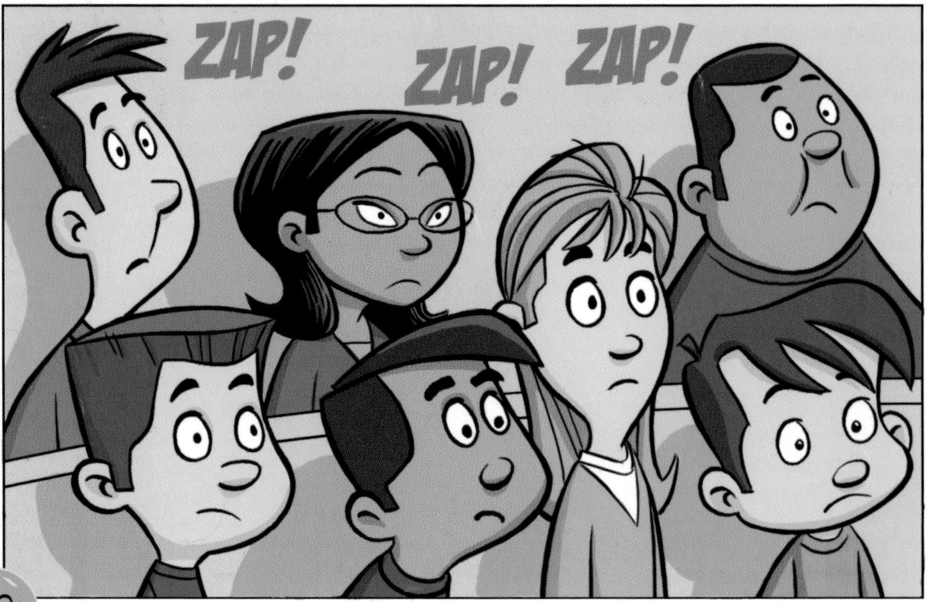
ZAP!
ZAP!
ZAP!

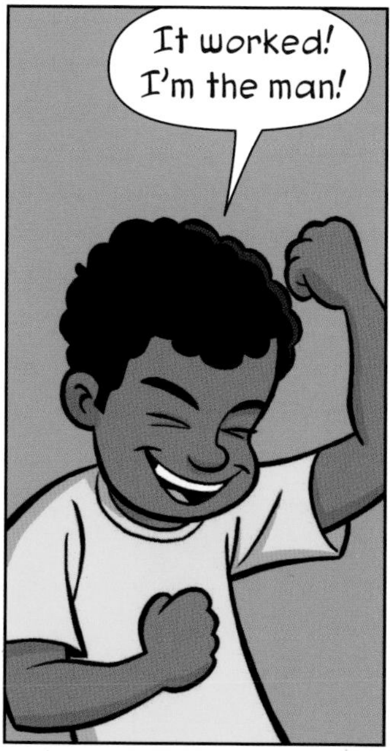
It worked! I'm the man!

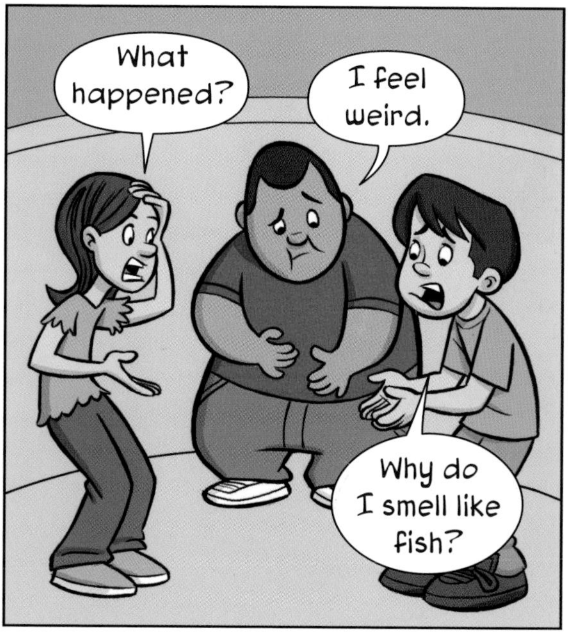
What happened?
I feel weird.
Why do I smell like fish?

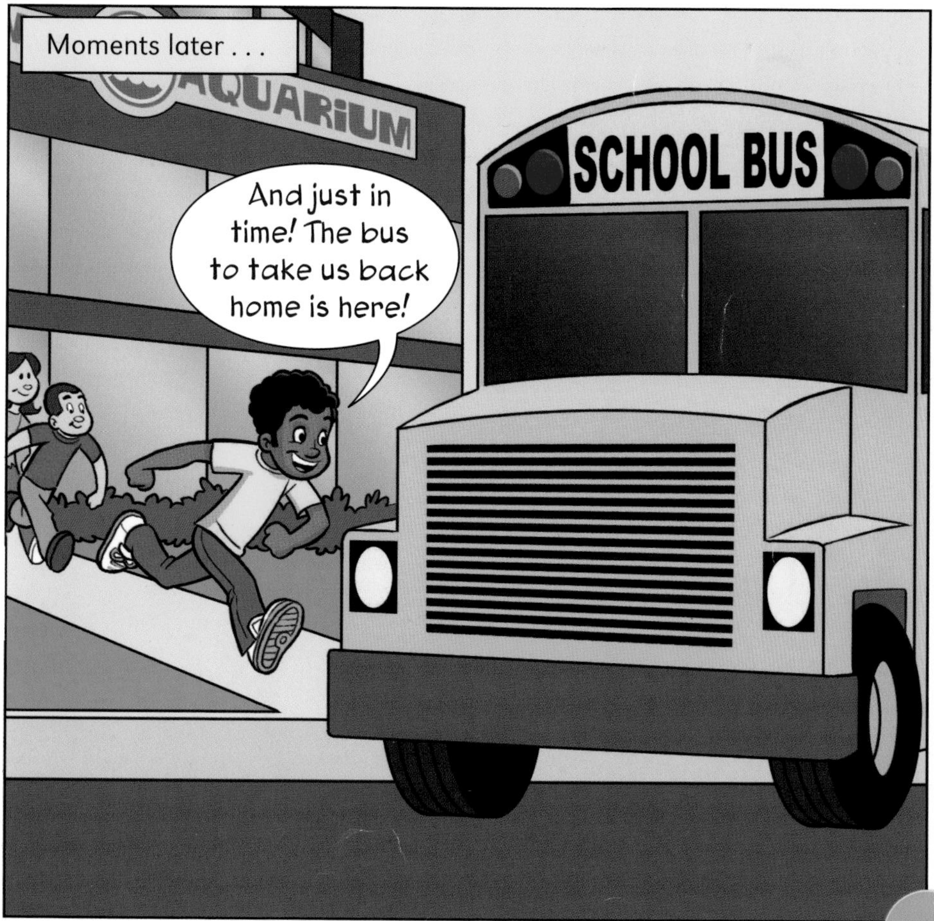
Moments later . . .
AQUARIUM
SCHOOL BUS
And just in time! The bus to take us back home is here!

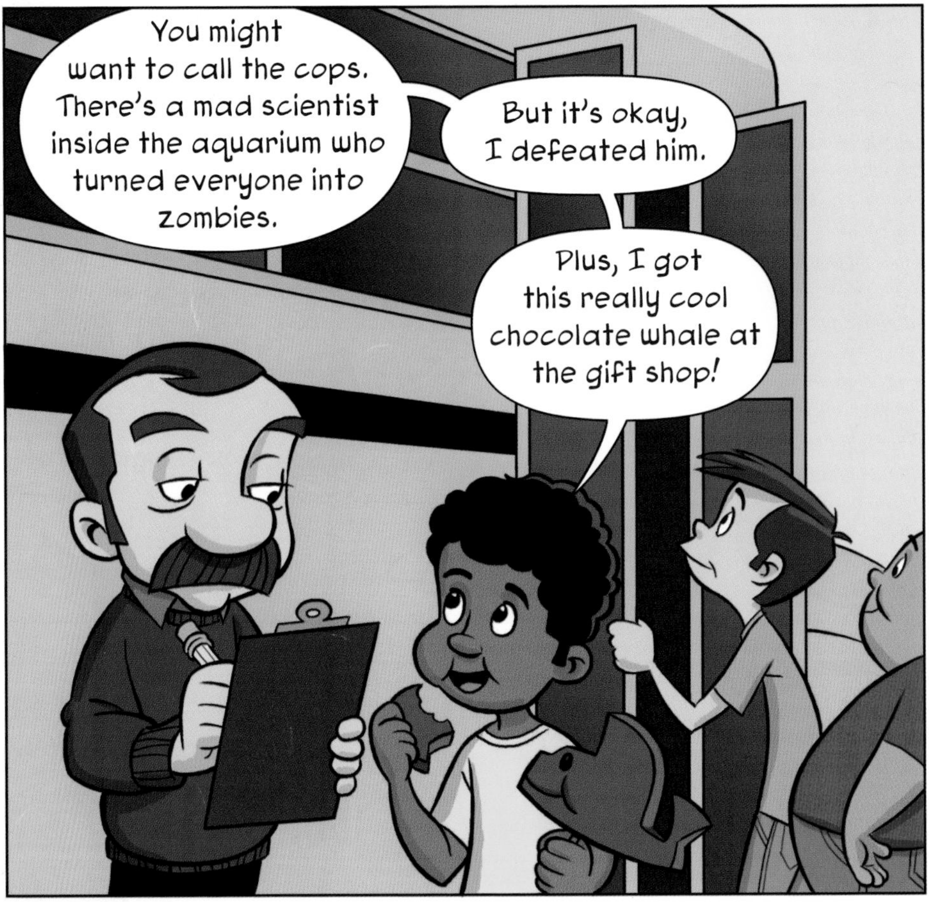
You might want to call the cops. There's a mad scientist inside the aquarium who turned everyone into zombies.
But it's okay, I defeated him.
Plus, I got this really cool chocolate whale at the gift shop!

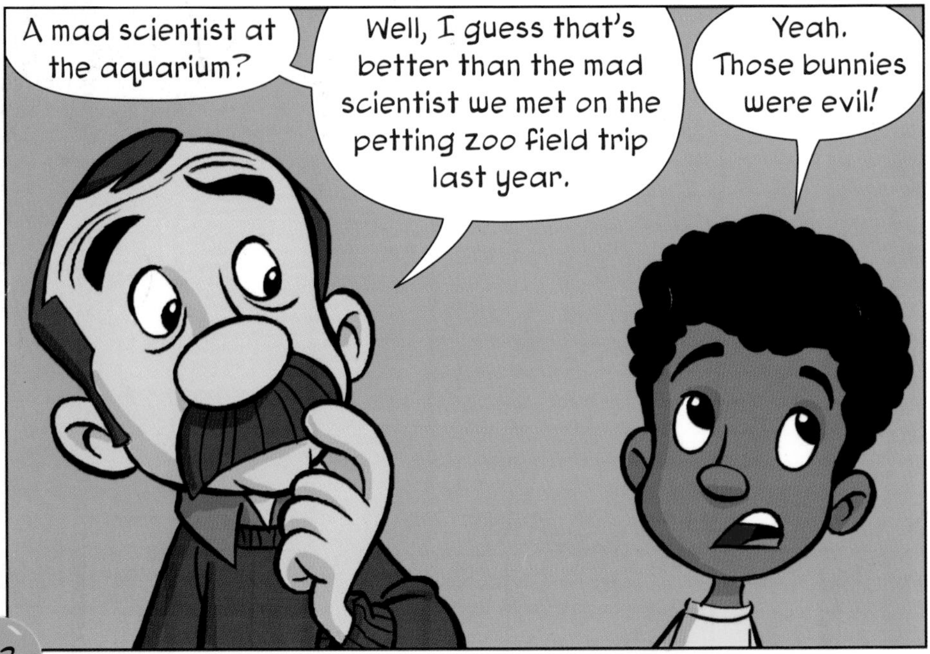
A mad scientist at the aquarium?
Well, I guess that's better than the mad scientist we met on the petting zoo field trip last year.
Yeah. Those bunnies were evil!

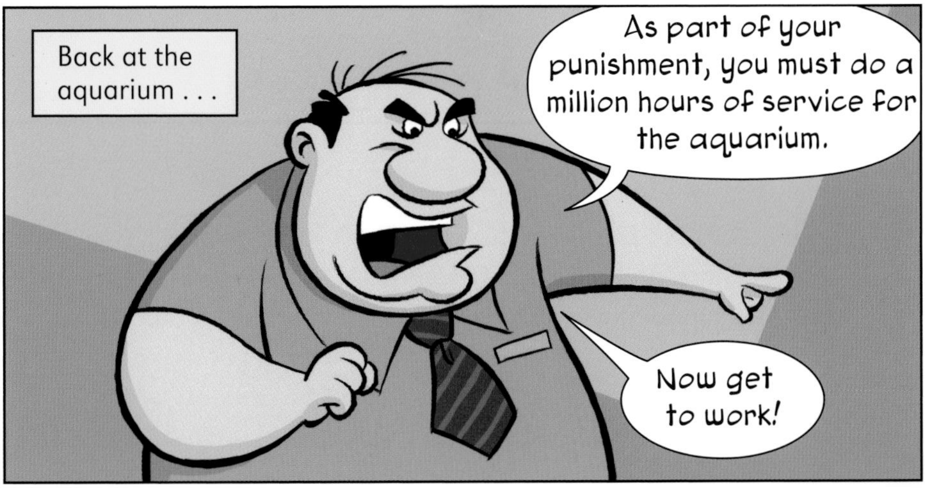
Back at the aquarium . . .
As part of your punishment, you must do a million hours of service for the aquarium.
Now get to work!

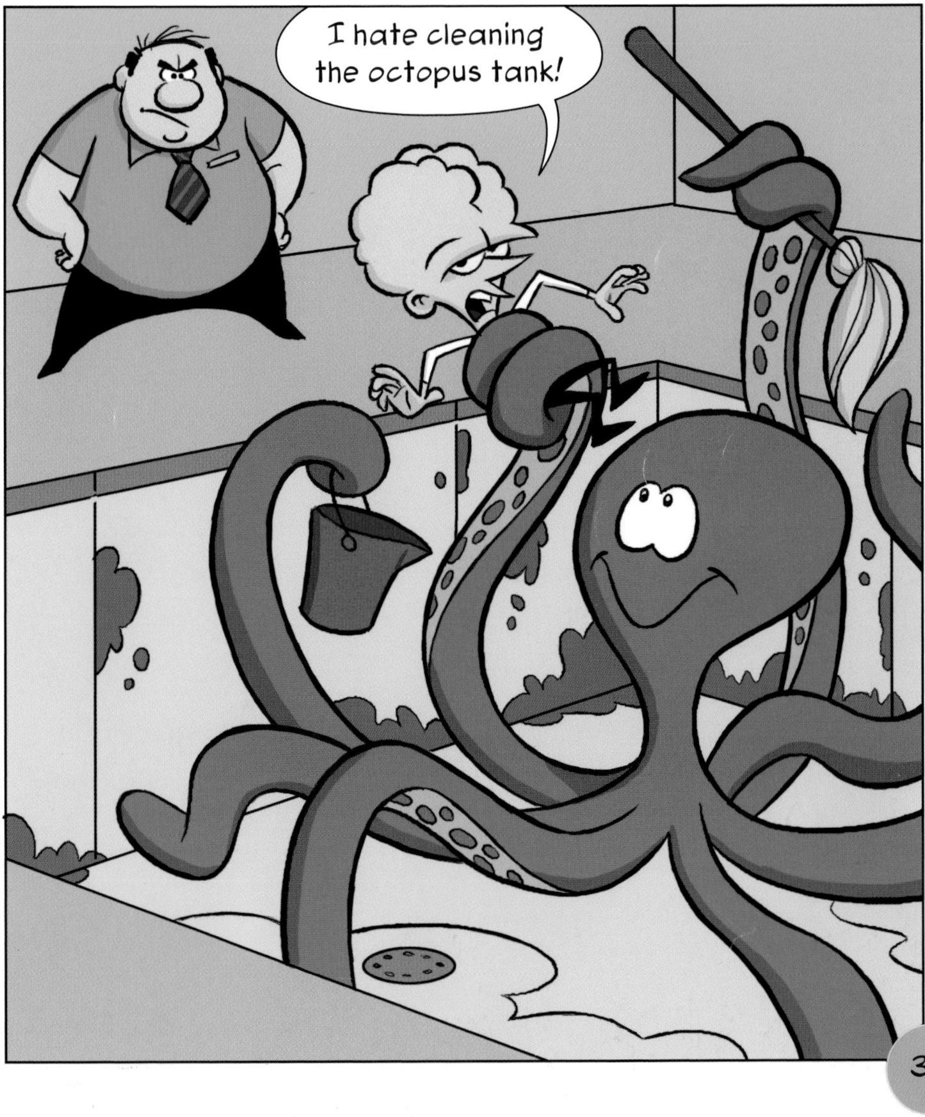
I hate cleaning the octopus tank!

ABOUT THE AUTHOR

Born in 1962 in Denver, Colorado, Scott Nickel works by day at Paws, Inc., Jim Davis's famous Garfield studio, and freelances by night. He has created hundreds of humorous greeting cards, and written several children's books, short fiction for *Boys' Life* magazine, comic strips, and lots of really funny knock-knock jokes. He was raised in Southern California. In 1995 Scott moved to Indiana, where he currently lives with his wife, two sons, six cats, and several sea monkeys.

ABOUT THE ILLUSTRATOR

Cedric Hohnstadt says he came to Earth in a rocket ship and was adopted by a kindly farm couple. Actually, he was born on September 16, 1972, in Mankato, Minnesota. Since 1996, Cedric has been a freelance illustrator, working with characters such as the Jetsons and Curious George. In 2000, he attended the Disney Institute summer program and caught the animation bug. Soon he was doing designs and storyboards for Focus on the Family Films. In 2005, Cedric married his lovely wife Jennie. They have one daughter.

GLOSSARY

acrobatics (ak-ruh-BAT-iks)—gymnastic moves, such as flips, handstands, and spins

aquarium (uh-KWAIR-ee-uhm)—a place where fish and water animals are kept for people to look at and learn about

Gettysburg Address (GEH-teez-burg uh-DRESS)—a famous speech given by U.S. President Abraham Lincoln on November 19, 1863. In this case, **address** means a speech, and not where someone lives.

professional (pruh-FESH-uh-nuhl)—someone good enough at an activity to make it a career. Acrobats and animal wranglers are professionals. Zombies are not!

scurvy (SKUR-vee)—a pirate word for something bad or stinky. Scurvy is also the name of a sickness that pirates would get if they didn't eat enough fresh fruit. True!

wrangler (RANG-guhl-uhr)—a person who herds or controls a group of animals

zombie (ZOM-bee)—someone whose brain is controlled by another person; when you tell your friend to eat worms, and he does it, he is acting like a zombie.

zombify (ZOM-buh-fye)—to turn someone into a zombie

ALL ABOUT AQUARIUMS

Ever seen a whale walking down the street or an octopus at the bus stop? Of course not. They live in the sea with millions of other animals and fish. Luckily, aquariums let everyone get close to underwater creatures. Here's a few facts about these amazing places:

In 1853, the world's first public aquarium (made with glass) opened in Regents Park, London. They called it — what else? — the Fish House.

Today, there are thousands of aquariums all over the world. The largest aquarium opened in Atlanta, Georgia, in November 2005. The Georgia Aquarium holds 8 million gallons of water, which could fill 160,000 bathtubs!

The Georgia Aquarium has more than 100,000 fish including whale sharks—the largest fish on earth. These giants can grow more than 50 feet long. That's bigger than a school bus!

Public aquariums aren't just a home for fish. Dolphins, sea otters, turtles, and even penquins are also some of the main attractions.

Ripley's Aquarium of the Smokies in Gatlinburg, Tennessee, has the longest underwater tunnel at 345 feet. Visitors can explore the see-through tunnel during the day. Or, if they dare, sleep beneath swimming sharks at night.

Want to get even closer to some sea life? At the Underwater Adventures Aquarium in Minnesota, visitors can **touch** real stingrays and even sharks!

Of course, you don't have to leave home to experience the beauty of tropical fish. Millions of people have aquariums in their home. In fact, aquarium fish are one of the most popular pets in America.

Fish are my favorite people!

DISCUSSION QUESTIONS

1.) Trevor ignored his group leader and went into the gift shop by himself. If he hadn't wandered off, Trevor might have become a zombie. Does this make his decision okay?

2.) Dr. Brainium uses the Zombitron 3000 to make some of his zombies solve math problems. Is brainwashing people to do good things all right? Why or why not?

3.) In the end, Dr. Brainium is forced to clean the octopus tank. Do you think this was a good punishment? How would you have punished him for turning the students into zombies?

WRITING PROMPTS

1.) Trevor and his class had a pretty wacky field trip. Write about your favorite field trip ever. Then, describe where you would like to go on the next field trip.

2.) Dr. Brainium is really smart, but he's also really evil. Why do you think he's such a mean guy? Write a story about Dr. Brainium's childhood and tell how he became the world's most evil scientist.

3.) If you had a Zombitron 3000 and could zombify animals, what animal would you want to control? Make a list of chores that you would make the animal do.

INTERNET SITES

Do you want to know more about subjects related to this book? Or are you interested in learning about other topics? Then check out FactHound, a fun, easy way to find Internet sites.

Our investigative staff has already sniffed out great sites for you!

Here's how to use FactHound:

1. Visit *www.facthound.com*

2. Select your grade level.

3. To learn more about subjects related to this book, type in the book's ISBN number: **1598898345**.

4. Click the **Fetch It** button.

FactHound will fetch the best Internet sites for you!